Dream a Little Dream

Eleanor Wagner

DEDICATION

My husband, Steve

and

My two daughters, Viktoria-Leigh and Kassidy

Also, by the author:
Sussex County Hauntings and Other Strange Phenomena
Sussex County Hauntings and Other Strange Phenomena: Part II
Warren County Hauntings and Other Strange Phenomena

Cover art by Traci Markou.

ACKNOWLEDGMENTS

This book is dedicated to three of my biggest supporters: My husband, Steve, who over twenty years ago told me to shoot for the stars, because I might be surprised where they'd take me, and my two daughters, Viktoria-Leigh and Kassidy. Tori – who encouraged me to pick up where I left off that long time ago and catch the shooting star, and Kassidy who was cheering me on the entire way!

I find Acknowledgements in a book are so important. They mustn't be overlooked. They're a personal, heartfelt thank you to people in your life who down the line inspired, encouraged, supported or aided you in some way to be able to put the words down on paper and get them to where they are now.

Anyone who knows me, knows I've been writing forever! They clearly remember the notes and pads of paper all over the place with jots here and there of words or thoughts which would one day end up in a poem or short story. I clearly recall the pad on my bedside table for those *in the middle of the night* moments when I awakened and quickly recorded a thought or idea I'd otherwise forget by morning. I vividly recall writing my very first poem in grade school. No surprise, it had to do with Halloween. I even did the illustrations of witches and ghouls all around the wording.

Nonetheless, this project began well over thirty years ago and in the various stages, I have my sister-in-law Ellen Dorian, to thank for taking the journey with me by reading chapter after chapter and kindly offering her feedback to completion. Once the book was done, feeling accomplished, into a box and storage it went. Gone, but certainly not forgotten.

Little did I know that many years later, Facebook would reunite me with high school friends where I would discover a former classmate and author in his own right, Mark McGrath. After finding out about his published book, Mark shared his publisher's information and encouraged me to submit my manuscript.

I unearthed the long-hidden manuscript. As I took out the storage box and wiped the dust off the top, I realized pages were missing and everything was on ancient floppy discs from the 90s. My husband Steve asked a co-worker for help with getting the information off the dinosaur floppy discs of yesteryear and succeeded.

The writing *itch* returned with a fervor I had long since packed away. Mark had reignited that burning drive to see the journey through to the end. So, thank you Mark for lighting the fire under my ass and forcing me to get over the fear of rejection.

To be able to say I've checked one off my bucket list is priceless. A smile curves my lips as I look at the notepad sitting atop my nightstand table.

Chapter One

The Survivor

Victoria Sheldon loved autumn in New Jersey. It was beautiful when the foliage glimmered a brilliant, burning red, deep brown and orange. But once winter rushed in, it was long and hard, forcing New Jersey inhabitants into hibernation for at least six months out of the year as nature began its tedious work of stripping the forest of its brightly colored leaves. Before long, they'd be bare, depicting a bitterness to match the climate.

She slowly walked in the darkness toward where she parked her car in the back lot of the theater. The front lot was almost full, but as she neared the back, she noticed fewer and fewer cars about.

Her eyes scanned the surrounding area, but her mind was still on the movie's surprise ending. The night was a cool, one of the first signs of fall leaving and winter making its grand entrance.

Victoria adjusted her jacket to her chest to keep out the incessant chill, and finally she decided to zip it up. Normally, she bickered about the weather, but tonight the coolness did nothing to dampen her spirits. Smiling, she stuck her hands into the pockets to keep them warm. She was glad she had gone to the movies, even though she was alone. Adam had another of his last-minute business meetings to attend, and it would run late, as usual.

During the three years of their marriage, she got used to *last-minute* meetings arising with regularity.

In order to fill the constant void of Adam's absence, she took up tennis and golf on weekends. In the evenings, reading a good book or renting a newly released DVD were typical selections. Occasionally, she'd embellish by having a night on her own of dinner and a movie. She was happy when her decision to do that tonight, especially since it was the premiere of the movie, *The Survivor*, starring her favorite actor, Kyran Cornell, a man to die for! Her heart pounded at the thought of his name, so much that it hurt. She felt like a young girl with a high school crush. Adam knew about her fondness for the actor, but she never intentionally rubbed it in his face as much as she would've liked to. It probably wouldn't have affected him in the least bit anyway. When the opportunity arose for her to see a movie in which he starred, she preferred going alone. This way she wouldn't have to subject Adam to all her oohing and aahing.

God forbid she should confess to Adam that Kyran was her fantasy man. What had been a minute crush in the beginning had progressed in magnitude. Not only did she fantasize about Kyran, but she dreamt of him often. She understood her reasons for having an emotional attachment to a celebrity she'd never met or known. It was to make up for what she lacked with Adam.

She closed her eyes and sucked in a breath of cool air, relishing in the substance of it. She jump-skipped a few steps in exclamation. She felt like a kid again. Every time she saw a movie, any movie, it had the same effect on her afterwards. It made her feel as though she didn't have a care in the world- no worries to think of. Logic told her it was mere fantasy, but it *was* fun to live it for a while, nonetheless.

Kyran was a spectacular looking man. There was no question about that. He wasn't one of those typical musclemen who worked out daily lifting weights, but he had a strong, sturdy physique and a perfectly proportioned bottom. His hair, naturally golden blonde, gave the impression of being bleached. His eyes were a deep, penetrating brown, and sparkled when looked at. They were captivating and suggested raw sexuality and sensitivity at the same time. He had inherited chubby cheeks from his famous father, a looker in his own right. To top it off, he was an excellent actor. Ten times better than his father; ten times better than anyone his age in the industry. He knew how to make the ladies swoon and the men respect him for it. Victoria was certain that with his track record to date, he'd be up for an Oscar in no time. All he needed was the right script. He was too exceptional not to be noticed.

What harm could there be in fantasizing?

She snapped out of her reverie, laughing aloud at her thoughts. She was busy concentrating on Kyran that she almost missed the row in which she parked her car. S-7. The only way she could remember it was by giving the row's letter a word she couldn't possibly forget.

S-7. Sex.

Sex-7.

Something she wouldn't forget. Something she didn't get enough of these days. Come to think of it, it was something she wasn't getting any of at all.

The letter/word system worked well for her. She could immediately summon up the letter and number straightaway. Before coming up with the idea, she usually wandered around parking lots senselessly in search of her car.

She reached the 'S' row and picked out her car parked alongside a red Nissan. Remembering the row didn't matter this time, because her car was one among only a few others along with a huge, gray dumpster which stood on the opposite end of the parking lot. Her fault all the same, because she hadn't immediately left the theater after the movie ended. She stopped to go to the bathroom, because she didn't want to get up during the movie and risk missing a good part. Now, the only moving car was several rows away. A Chevy Silverado pulled out with its radio blaring so loudly that a rhythmic rumble loud enough to wake the dead was heard through its closed windows. Other cars parked there were silent and empty, their previous occupants already gone in for the late show. She was alone.

Her mood was upbeat as she walked over to her car: a 2007, charcoal-gray Hyundai. Not a rich woman's sports car, but economical and reliable. It suited her needs perfectly. A few cars passed her by, heading toward the parking lot exit. Victoria was humming the theme song from the movie as she reached into her handbag to pull out her key ring. A heart-shaped key holder engraved with hers and Adam's name jangled as she picked out the correct key. Looking at it brought back the memory of how she hemmed and hawed until Adam gave in and bought it for her. He hadn't wanted to buy it but did so because she made such a fuss. She should've picked up on his attitude then, but she was blinded by her own emotions and never once suspected his feelings were false.

She remembered the incident all too well. The fun-loving joy of game-playing she felt when was now nothing more than longing for what could've been.

Nevertheless, she would make the best of things as she always did.

She reached out to slip the key into the lock. The attack was sudden and swift. Victoria didn't even see it coming.

She barely caught a glimpse of a shadow whooshing toward her. The man apparently circled around the back of the car. He wrapped one arm around her neck, proffering a sharp-bladed knife in the other, wasting no time.

"Shut up or I'll kill you," he said, holding her tightly from behind.

His voice, brash and raspy, was slightly accented but indistinguishable. The blade he held gleamed under the parking lot's lamplight.

"I'll take away my hand, but I want you to get in the car without screamin' or else you're a dead woman, comprende?"

He was unusually strong.

"Y-Yes," she managed to respond.

She wondered if he could feel her body shaking, if he could sense her fear. She remained docile and compliant.

He slowly released his hand and forced her into the car from the driver's side onto the passenger seat.

Victoria trembled. Her heart was pounding in her chest.

"Why are you doing this?" she whispered, terrified beyond reason. "T-Take my money. Take the car, but please let me go."

She heard about carjacking, but never believed she'd fallen victim to it. The neighborhood was a good one, not subject to much crime. Experience made her strong enough to endure many things, but nothing so unexpected as this.

She conjured up a different strategy.

"Please don't hurt me. I'm pregnant," she said, trying to sound frail.

Would he be sympathetic? She hoped he would.

He sneered.

"Gimme the keys, bitch," he said, grabbing them from her extended hand. His voice was deep and gruff. "Don't try anything smart. Remember, I've got the knife. You try fightin' me, and I'll stick you good."

He shoved the knife under her chin. When he saw he'd gotten his point across, he took it away.

He turned on the ignition, looking for the switch to the lights, and pulled out of the parking lot onto the road heading west, all the while keeping one eye on her. Michael Buble softly singing the lyrics to "Dream a Little Dream of Me" emanated from the car stereo. The man flicked the switch off.

Victoria was at the disadvantage. *Where is everybody now?* She thought. Moments ago, dozens of people were walking to their cars after leaving the same theater. *Why the hell did I have to park so far in the back section? Because you arrived at the theater too late to find decent parking up front. That's why!* She answered herself. *And just because it's well-lit doesn't make it safe. Dumb. What you did was dumb.*

She looked around frantically, a feeling of desperation and fear enveloped her. Her only hope had been a black blazer making a turn at the corner of the intersection. No other moving cars could be seen.

My God! What the hell do I do now? Her attacker made it perfectly clear what would happen if she tried fleeing. She could smell her own fear, the mixture of sweat and body odor intertwining. She struggled to hold in the tears but failed. She scanned the car for a weapon but didn't see anything useful. She wished she wasn't such a neat freak. Maybe if she'd been a slob, she would've kept all sorts of garbage lying around in the car that might've been useful as a weapon. No sense in thinking about that now though. *Watch where he's driving instead*, she reminded herself. *Backtrack later if necessary.*

"You don't want to do this," she tried reasoning with him.

"Shut up," he said flatly.

"You can let me go, and I won't say anything," she attempted further, hoping it wouldn't anger him.

By the tone of his voice, she was getting the impression he wouldn't stand for her blabbering comments much longer.

"Shut up," he said again.

After a minute or so, she managed to smother her sobbing sounds, but hot tears still ran freely down the sides of her cheeks, blurring her vision. She would've wiped them away but was afraid to move for fear of startling him into doing something drastic. She didn't want to ruin any chances she might have of escape.

"No one will ever have to know," she said in desperation.

When dealing with a criminal, you had to think like one, but it appeared as if he tuned her out completely.

"I said shut up," he snarled in between clenched teeth.

"But I don't even know who you are."

She almost stopped herself from saying this, because she could tell he was beginning to get on his nerves.

"Shut the *fuck* up! Shut up! Shut up! Shut up!" he screeched.

He grabbed her hair, holding a clump of it between his fingers along with the knife.

"Ahhhh," she cried, swallowing bile.

She couldn't help groaning as he tugged harder.

"Did you hear what I said?" he screamed.

Victoria's eyes bulged from their sockets. She managed a nod, and he let go of her. She settled herself back again. Her negligence produced a close call that could've cost her her life. Who knows what he might've done if he totally lost it.

What if....

Victoria snuck a glance at the speedometer gauge. He was following the speed limit, moving steadily at forty miles per hour. He hunched over slightly, squinting his eyes to get a clearer view of the road ahead. The defogger wasn't working very well. Neither was the heater. Victoria felt chilled to the bone. The car jolted with a bumping sound after running over potholes in the road. She hoped he wouldn't get on the highway anytime soon. *I'll distract him or draw attention to another vehicle on the road.*

She glanced down at the glowing, red numbers on the digital clock. Given the time, close to midnight on a weeknight, the likelihood that many people would be out and about was slim. She knew that, in most cases as this, the victims never made it out alive. Her odds weren't very good unless she came up with a plan, and quick.

Her aggressor was visibly nervous; sweating profusely. Occasionally, he'd press the hand which held his weapon against his forehead as if pained by a headache. Any swift movement could prove fatal.

He might not hurt me, she hoped.

It was possible he was running from something or someone and needed a getaway car. She immediately discarded that idea.

Stop kidding yourself about getting out of this alive. This creep is the worst of the worst.

His treatment of her clearly indicated he wouldn't think twice about killing her. If she waited any longer, giving him the opportunity to get on the highway, he'd take her someplace secluded and she'd be dead meat. The motion of the car and the steady humming of its tires reverberated through her body.

Too late. As she finished summing up her options, the car turned onto the highway. It started to rain. Dirty water bulleted the Hyundai's windshield. The man took his eyes off the road briefly to glance at her. She stiffened in her seat, and he looked away. Victoria sat up straight, breathing fast and fervently. Her palms were damp with perspiration. She needed to calm down.

Be alert, she ordered herself.

Silence.

The silence was deadening. She'd be more comfortable talking, feeling him out. He was visibly apprehensive, darting his eyes around the area every few seconds, pushing the car as fast as he dared on the slippery roadway. He kept the knife in clear view, clearly ready to use it if he had to. Victoria watched the signs and landmarks, making mental notes for her planned escape. There was a patch of swamp land on the right, and a row of woods on the left. Red taillights swiftly receded into the night.

She sketched a mental description of her assailant: Mid-thirties. Aquiline nose, thick lips, and wiry, black hair. Possibly Hispanic, but she couldn't be sure. His beard was streaked with gray. He had sharp, black eyes that undressed you while scanning over your body. Broad shoulders, broader than average and built like an ox; a muscular build. Stubby fingers with nails chewed down to the pulp, bleeding on some. At that moment, she was quite proud of herself. If she wasn't just short of shitting in her pants, she could pat herself on the shoulder for her careful, detailed observation.

She decided quickly she couldn't forget him even if she wanted to. His face would remain embedded in her mind forever. *So much for detailed observation!* He succeeded in frightening her beyond repair, and by attacking her, he induced a fierce streak of anger such that she was stunned by its magnitude. By memorizing his face, she'd get her revenge.

You wait, you bastard, she thought. *You're going to be sorrier than ever for picking me for a target!* Victoria never felt such a powerful need for revenge. She was sick of being taken advantage of. It happened all too often in her life. When she was younger and being abused, she was helpless to do anything but hide inside herself. Not anymore. Her body was taut and aggressive, ready to do battle.

A road sign warned of an approaching curve. The man guided the car through the sharp left-hand turn and then back again to the right. Light bounced off the fog, casting blinding reflections.

After a half-hour of highway driving, the man pulled the car off at an exit without a street sign. The remote area was unfamiliar to her. Her gaze swept the surrounding mountainside. There were fewer and fewer isolated houses along the stretch. Before long, there was only a vast expanse of wilderness and rock. Victoria's was the only car in sight on either side of the divided road.

Think fast, she urged herself.

No streetlamps lit the perimeter ahead. A forest of trees surrounded the winding road. The storm quieted and shirked its maddening force. A slow rain was now hitting the windshield in a spray of droplets. The car's bright lights illuminated a sign which read, Welcome to *Wawayanda State Park*. They swept on past without turning. The road was rough and potholed in some areas, making the road a bumpy one, but he drove the car with skill, guiding the car through left-hand and right-hand turns with extreme ferocity.

If she somehow broke free, and didn't sustain much injury in the interim, she'd run like a bandit. She noted that he was slowing down to forty miles per hour again. *Probably doesn't want to draw any unwanted attention*, she thought. Not that there were any cars out. An occasional one approached, but nothing was behind them. That didn't matter. Victoria was certain he would take every precaution no matter what the circumstance. From everything so far, it was clear this guy was no novice to his trade.

They traveled approximately two miles on the tightly packed, mountainous road, dark shadows at every curve. Trees rose up on all sides. *They must be a part of the state park we passed a while ago*, she thought. They passed another road sign that indicated they were six miles from any kind of civilization.

She contemplated the situation at hand. *I must do something*, she reasoned, trying to summon up the courage to follow through with the plan she concocted.

Go. Go. Go.

She didn't want to let her eagerness overtake her, because then she would undoubtedly make a mistake, and she couldn't bear that.

What in God's name are you thinking of doing? she asked herself sternly, and replied in the same mental breath, *the only sane thing possible.*

He won't be able to find me in the dark, she assured herself. *I can run zigzag, stopping every now and again to listen for him following.*

Yes. That's what I'll do.

Thank God she hadn't habitually fastened her seat belt. What would she have done then?

She turned her head slightly, pretending to peer out the window. Out of the corner of her eye, she stole a quick look at the door lock. It was open. For once, she was grateful for her forgetfulness! She waited another moment and rechecked the speedometer. Still forty miles per hour.

Do it! She urged herself. *Do it now!*

Choking back fear, she shoved the door open, and threw herself out.

Chapter Two

It was getting late, and Adam Sheldon knew he should get ready to go home. Victoria would be arriving home shortly after going to the late show at the theater, and he wanted to get there before she did if he could.

Adam smiled at the thought of how Victoria believed him totally when he told her he had to work late. She was so damned naïve. What he was really doing was involving himself in a sexual rendezvous, something he indulged in frequently since he couldn't get satisfaction from home.

His most recent one started six months ago with his boss's wife, Lina. She stopped in to see her husband. On her way out to the elevator, Adam caught up with her and conveniently introduced himself, expecting a handshake and a few perfunctory words, but instead found himself invited to join her for lunch. He jumped on the offer. It was so easy. Better yet, she was pleasantly well-endowed, and rich to boot.

They went to Ciaobella Restaurant on Third Avenue in Manhattan, taking a booth in the far corner. It was a place she knew well, and where everyone knew her. Discretion wasn't one of her better traits. Lina felt blunt openness would conceal the true nature of their relationship. They would appear to be socializing friends for mere business associates.

She chose to sit next to him, which was as indiscreet as you could get. She ordered for them both. Martinis to start. Strong ones.

The first martini got them into heavy conversation. The second one produced a heavy petting scene. After their third martini, she was fondling his penis underneath the table. And once the main course arrived, they were indecently disposed. She paid the bill, and they left without touching a bite. In room 619 of the Hyatt, they finished what they had started. From then on, it became steady trade.

This evening had been no different than the rest. They just completed a rough evening of sex and booze. Adam was feeling warm and high.

Lina was wearing her Get-Lost-I'm-Through-With-You-For-Tonight look where she sucked in her mouth and dropped her sleepy eyes disgustedly, sighing in discontent. It always made Adam feel inferior, and he didn't like it. He was used to being in control, the powerful one, but with Lina it was different and had been since the beginning. Adam supposed it was one of the things which attracted him to her. He couldn't understand his double standards. Lina thrived on being the dominator, even during sex, which was without a doubt a turn-on for Adam. But whenever she acted like this after a wild bout of lovemaking, Adam felt as though he hadn't been good enough, that he hadn't satisfied her fully.

Annoyed, he got up and went into the bathroom to take a piss. While he was taking care of business, he thought about how sneaking around with his boss's wife was exciting, but the fact that pleasing her was always such an infinite challenge was even more so. It made him try harder.

Victoria was too easy. She never complained; appeared to be fulfilled every time and was never a challenge whatsoever. With Lina, there was never any pleasing her. No matter how hard he tried, she always finished off with the same off-handed expression. Adam supposed the affair would last as long as the challenge existed for him.

He sauntered back into the hotel room acting as if her reaction didn't faze him in the least. He never let on that she succeeded in pinching a nerve, but remained calm and composed, forever *The Man*. This seemed to make her mad and try harder, and it got him horny again. He desperately wanted to go down on her one more time, but it really was getting late. He didn't want Victoria to become suspicious, because lately she was proving to be smarter than he thought, and he felt she might finally have an idea that something was up. But there wasn't any sense in being obvious about it. Although she never questioned him or called his job to check up on him, he didn't want to take any chances.

Lina was busy pulling her stockings on over her panties. Braless, her tits bobbed up and down as she bounced to stretch the hose up tightly. He watched her as she completed the hose and went for the bra. She finished snapping it and was going for her leopard skin blouse when Adam snuck up behind her, roughly grabbing a hold of her breast, biting the side of her neck.

"Adam," she hummed without an ounce of pleasure. "Give it a rest. Harvey's waiting for me at home."

She and Harvey Kosen had been married for ten years. "He already thinks I'm out doing charity work and that only takes so much time."

She'd done it again; managed to make him feel unattractive. Adam was annoyed, but aroused, nonetheless.

Why is it whenever we first get into the room together, she's like a cat in heat, screeching and clawing her way at my clothes, never getting enough, riding like wildfire until we're spent? Then, she acts like it wasn't anything special.

The combination of the challenge and his thoughts made him hard again.

"No kidding," he flatly responded, not letting on that she'd gotten the best of him again. "I've got one waiting at home, too. Remember?"

Fetching for a dig of his own, he added, "And I know she'll be expecting me to perform my husbandly functions."

His voice was stinging. He turned and smirked, awaiting her reaction, knowing well-enough it was a lie. Victoria never made the first move. If she did, maybe they'd have a better sex life.

"Well, don't overdo the performance," she responded, clearly a tinge affected. "I'm the one you aim to please, and don't forget it."

Her eyebrows rose in dry amusement. As if to get in his good graces, she went over and French-kissed him, slowly humping up and down his leg, trying to stimulate him, breathing heavily as she did so.

Bingo! It was working. His manhood rose fully to the attention. She immediately stopped and laughed.

"I'll bet she can't do that no matter how hard she tries," she said, sudden passion in her voice.

"M-m-m-m," he responded, forgetting totally about his rush to get home, ready to perform for her in top form.

She pulled away.

"Another time, Adam," she stated. "Can't make Harvey suspicious. He's not as naïve as yours is. Besides, I've got my own duties to perform."

Whore, he thought. *She has to have the last word; get in the last dig.*

"Gotta run."

She grabbed for her coat and bag, slipped into her high-heeled pumps, and smacked a small one on his sore lips. They were sore after every episode with Lina, and there had been a lot of them lately. They couldn't seem to get enough of one another. Adam hoped the challenge would last. He felt it might. Lina rushed through the door, letting it close abruptly behind her, leaving Adam standing alone. He dressed and left for home.

***

Victoria landed headlong on the asphalt roadway, smacking her head several times before bouncing in and out of a ditch and down a steep incline. She tumbled and rolled for what seemed like an eternity, knocking the breath from her and flinging bits of dust and rock into her face along the way. Finally, she came to an abrupt stop at the bottom of an embankment. Her side stung from a wound inflicted by the knife prior to escaping.

The son of a bitch managed to get me, she realized, breathing in quick, shallow gusts of air. She gingerly examined the wound. It ached to the touch. The smells of her sweat-soaked body and blood drenched shirt intermixing made her want to vomit.

There isn't much time, she reminded herself.

She heard a frantic scream of brakes and squeal of tires in the distance, and staggered to her feet, gasping for more air to silence her racing heart. Her head was spinning. She felt as though an invisible hand slapped her face. It burned terribly, and she could tell there were scratches.

The roar of the engine sounded as the car turned around and headed in her direction. The thunderous squeal of tires forced her into action.

I need to move fast!

Shaky and weak-kneed, she pulled herself up, holding onto her bleeding shoulder, and dragged herself a few feet. Odd smoky shapes wafted in the cold, night air. She surveyed the area around her but could see nothing but darkness.

You're going to have to run, you idiot, she told herself. *If you're going to make any headway, you need to run!*

Run for your life!

And she did.

The area was a mass of rock slopes. Her shoulder ached terribly. Blood soaked through her new denim shirt. She was gradually getting dizzy. Her head throbbed. She put her hand to her head, feeling wetness. She forced herself forward, bolting about frantically, falling over trees and rocks in her path. She couldn't see two feet in front of her, but her sense of smell informed her she was in an all-encompassing world of birch, oak and pine. Visibility was zero. The darkness was overwhelming. A distant night owl sounded its presence. Like a blind person, she waved her hands in front of her from right to left continuously, clawing away at the darkness.

She was a fighter, and she didn't plan on giving up easily. Whenever she faced a difficult situation, she drew on strength from within. Most importantly, she had the will to live. Until this moment, it never dawned on her how much her life meant to her. She would do whatever it took to keep it.

Stopping briefly to catch her breath, she realized she was losing an immense amount of blood and was slowly losing consciousness. She hugged herself and shivered, determined not to faint. With terror stripped of all reason, she felt if she closed her eyes, she would never awaken again. The metallic smell of blood filled the air. Her thoughts were flickering out with each passing second.

If I'm going to die, she thought, *I'd rather be here in this all-enveloping black hole than at the hands of that madman.*

***

Emilio couldn't believe what happened.

The Bitch jumped, he marveled, his black eyes wide and startled.

He never imagined she would give him the slip. Uh-uh. No way, Jose. He had to stop and look for her. He didn't cater to the idea of having to chase her down in the woods.

YOU DAMNED FOOL, Crater hammered from within the recesses of Emilio's mind. *NO LOOSE ENDS, REMEMBER? YOU CAN'T LET HER GET AWAY. FIND HER! MAKE HER PAY. TORMENT HER. TORTURE HER. YEAH. BRUTAL. EVER SO GENTLY BRUTAL.*

"Shut up!" Emilio shrieked. Crater was distracting him. *I'm not stupid*, he reminded himself.

He didn't plan on leaving behind loose ends. Too many people were looking for him already. Hopping from town to town, he left a trail of dead bodies in his wake, many of them unknown. He buried them in unmarked graves along the way, and those had never been discovered. Emilio had long since stopped counting how many he killed, and although Crater was responsible for the highest percentage of them, Emilio had been the one to carry out each grizzly task.

He was a wanted man. Emilio was surprised and a little disappointed he hadn't seen his face on *America's Most Wanted* or some true crime show yet. He came close to getting caught once in Cincinnati, but alerted by an ex-con friend, he had been long gone by the time the cops reached his hideout. Since then, they hadn't been able to sniff him out. The embarrassed, exasperated police force continually failed to catch him. Emilio Rodriguez was too devious and too sly. He smirked at the thought.

He was a drifter and had been one since running away from a dysfunctional home when he was thirteen, after being in and out of juvenile halls his entire life. Being on his own was a lot better. He did what he pleased, when he pleased.

At first, petty crimes kept him alive, but once he got involved with drugs and booze, his life changed dramatically. It was an entirely different ball game.

At fourteen, he met up with a fast-moving crowd, and they taught him the ropes. There wasn't a trick in the trade Emilio didn't know about. The gang members introduced him to plenty of kinky shit: animal offerings, rape, even cannibalism. He'd gotten a fondness for the taste of blood.

Over the years, deep within the confines of his brain, when Crater was nothing but a miniscule tumor in development, an intransigent fury was forming. Mental degeneration was imminent, and dark violence erupted, steering him aimlessly.

At sixteen, he ventured out on his own and started looking for blood himself. It wasn't hard. Naïve and trusting people were a dime a dozen. It was always a piece of cake. Before killing his victims, he befriended them, putting on a false face to gain their trust.

He was twenty-one when Crater entered the picture. Emilio started taking whatever he wanted by sheer force. Crater taught him how to do it and showed him it was alright.

The fury and Crater were urgent necessities in order to hang onto the last shred of sanity within himself. The two combined were the only strongholds enabling him to survive, his explanation for fulfilling the constant demand of his need; a focus on reaching his destiny. He became convinced of the necessity and importance in taking such forms of action.

Oh, he learned a lot from Crater, that much was certain, but lately he was sure he was outsmarting even Crater in the intelligence department. Crater's habit of taking too many unnecessary risks had gotten Emilio into trouble too often. Recently, he made the more rational decisions in order to guarantee their safety.

After turning the car around, he retraced the direction in which they had come, stopping at the spot he though the woman had fallen. He couldn't really tell for sure. His vision hadn't been good through the rearview mirror. All the trees looked the same. There weren't any landmarks to refer to for help in the location.

YOU FUCKED UP, ASSHOLE! Crater bellowed. *IF ANYONE PUTS US IN THE HOLE, IT'S YOU!*

"I said shut up!" Emilio screeched in a demented rage.

He never knew how to handle it when Crater talked down to him.

Chapter Three

Kyran Cornell jolted up in bed, shaking the blanket loose, knocking the novel onto the carpet where it lay open to the last page he'd been reading before falling asleep. His breathing was rapid and strained, his body soaked in sweat. The room was in total darkness except for the moonlight shimmering in between the mini blinds at the window. Shadows loomed along the walls.

His latest conquest lay beside him fast asleep. Julia Beckett, his co-star in the movie, *The Survivor*. She came home with him right after the movie's premiere the night before.

Why had he slept with her? Kyran wasn't sure.

He'd been doing a lot of one-nighters during the last three years. He hadn't been able to maintain a steady, meaningful relationship, and one-nighters were the next best thing. The bright lights of the city, bar hopping, and frolicking with women helped to soothe him, but didn't solve the long-range problem. He continually cautioned himself to slow down on the nightly sexcapades. He kept telling himself that once he found the right woman, he would. He wondered if that would ever happen.

The Dream, which came regularly every night, was responsible for his behavior of the past three years.

In The Dream, he's always with the same woman. They don't merely have sex. They make love. Kyran didn't know how he could tell the difference, but somehow, he knew. Day after day, night after night, week after week, The Dream pattern played itself out, the place and scenery the only thing changing. One night, they'd be doing it on a boat in the water under the stars. Yet, another night, it'd be on a sandy beach instead, right on the shoreline as the tide moved swiftly in and out.

As he lay under the warmth of his covers, Kyran could almost smell the sweetness of her as he remembered nuzzling her neck. He was breathless. His hand gently meandering to the nape of her neck, down to her breast where it lingered, gently squeezing. His hot breath blowing against her ear, his finger gliding to her bellybutton, around to her sensitive bottom, relishing each moment, wanting it to last forever. Whispering sweet nothings, prompting excited sighs and moans of pleasure; their lips touching, teasingly, getting more demanding until they reached a united sharpness. The distinct taste of her tongue upon his remained. In his mind, her sticky, moist body still caressed his, driving him crazy.

Looking over at Julia's spread-eagled form, he suddenly got a bad taste in his mouth, momentarily destroying the lingering memories of The Dream. He snuggled deeper under the blanket, turning on his side facing away from the woman beside him, and closed his eyes. He was ashamed of his attitude but couldn't do anything about it.

The Woman wasn't spectacularly gorgeous. He wouldn't compare her to any of the Hollywood starlets, but that's what he loved about her. She was a natural beauty, the kind that looked great without using makeup. Shoulder-length, blonde hair and remarkable hazel eyes framed her features. Her body was tall, lithe and tanned.

Whether The Woman was a figment of his imagination or not, Kyran was unsure, but he was obsessed nonetheless. The Dream was an addiction he couldn't do without. It shot through his system like pure cocaine did to a junkie. He couldn't wait for his next *fix*. Wakefulness confronted him with endless thoughts of The Mysterious Woman, and an eagerness and craving for the night to come, so he could enter in the throes of sleep and relive The Dream again in a different setting. He wondered. Would it be a mountaintop under the blue sky and white clouds? Or, in a Jacuzzi surrounded by knee-deep snow?

Eventually, The Woman taunted his mind during the day, as well. Fantasies about the torrid love they made together filled his mind. There was a strange realization that they belonged together.

Kyran wasn't an irrational person. Neither was he an irresponsible one. Unlike his fellow actor friends, he was clean and sober. There was a time in his life when he experimented with drugs and alcohol. In show-business, it was basically expected if you wanted to be looked at as a *somebody*. During his teen years into his early twenties, when he finally decided on becoming an actor, he hobnobbed with the rich and famous, attending one social engagement after another, each more lavishly prepared than the next. All of them served cocaine like it was an hors d'oeuvres. He lived an extravagant lifestyle, using it but never liking it.

After establishing himself in the industry and proving to the world he was a serious actor, he gave drugs up altogether. The fun of the parties and the glamour of the business began to fade. Kyran made up his mind if the hobnobby snobs didn't like it, they could all go to hell. He wasn't going to wreck his career and be labeled a has-been like most actors did after becoming full-fledged alkies or druggies. Now that he was thirty, he wasn't the least bit sorry about his decision.

Naturally, when The Dream began, he thought nothing of it, shrugging it off as a wet dream until it started coming on with overwhelming regularity. Then, he began to think differently. He suspected he might slowly be losing his mind, and it frightened him. He decided to attempt resolving the problem on his own. There was no way he'd go to a psychiatrist. If the tabloids got wind of the information, his reputation and career could be ruined. He worked too hard and came to far to risk losing it.

As time went on, The Dream became more demanding and insistent. He'd wake with the urgent need to release himself if he hadn't already done so in his sleep. Eventually, he surrendered full force. He'd gone with the flow and fulfilled the constant physical need that came with it by having one-nighters. This wasn't difficult in his profession. He easily found a willing partner, because he was well-known and popular in the industry. He wasn't proud of his actions. It made him dislike himself.

Tonight, for the first time in three years, The Dream had changed. Instead of wild lovemaking, The Woman was in imminent danger. Every time he came close to reaching her, she'd disappear and a frantic search to locate her ensued. The notion that danger was nearby and moving faster persisted, and Kyran became frenzied with saving her in time.

His fear for The Woman reached such intensity that upon waking, it left his body numb.

He sat up in his silk-sheeted bed, in the total darkness, and was afraid. He was at a loss about what to do. Could this sudden change mean he was reaching the breaking point and nearing insanity? Or, did The Woman exist and somewhere out in the vast world was in danger? And, most importantly, would he be able to find her?

***

Only when Victoria thought she distanced herself enough did she break to take another breather. Her lungs struggled to heave air in strong, hungry gulps. Her breath came out in brutal heaves, and she struggled to quiet them. She had the crazy notion he could hear her labored breathing and loud thumping heart. She lay motionless for fear that the slightest movement would give her location away.

Don't think about it. Just relax. Stand still. Don't. Don't....

She held her breath and listened for an ominously long amount of time.

The unseasonably cold weather temporarily lifted, and the rain stopped for the time being. Victoria wasn't sure how long it would let up. The clouds were moving in fast, dark and gray. Rain would slow down her progress. She hesitantly turned and looked behind her to see whether he was following her. She couldn't tell for certain, but somehow knew he was. She couldn't see him, but she heard him and swore he was coming fast, right behind her. She found herself nervously twitching at every sound and straining her eyes in the darkness to detect any movement. This brief encounter with death made her take a good look at herself.

She realized what survival meant to her. If she did survive this turmoil, her life would change. It already took a dramatic turn because of the night's events. Tumbles of unanswered questions swirled in her mind. A specific one popped up constantly: Why don't I have any friends? Why am I by myself all the time?

Adam.

It irrevocably trailed back to him. The realization forced her to reflect on her life. Adam didn't do much of anything with her, and he didn't like her having friends. She was in this mess because of him. Granted, she went out alone; of her own free will, but she did most everything on her own anyway. When she wanted to do things with Adam, he seemed disinterested. There was an excuse or reason for not going anyplace Victoria suggested. She was always giving in and doing what he wanted.

Sweet, simple, shy, complacent Victoria.

After they married, the only thing that changed was that she became a sweet, simple, shy and complacent wife.

Adam relentlessly forced submission to his desires, but she wouldn't submit any longer. She swore never again to be a woman who stayed home playing happy housewife.

Adam was accustomed to being dominant in all aspects of his life. As far as sex was concerned, they did it once in a blue moon, when the need struck him. When they did do it, it was because it was the normal thing to do, totally lacking romance and foreplay. She gave up on Adam a long time ago as far as sex was concerned. With him, it was wham-bam-thank-you-ma'am. Sure, she took care of Adam's needs, but he never seemed to care about hers. She turned to fantasy and masturbation for ultimate fulfillment.

Why hadn't she taken a closer notice at the way he was in the beginning? She took for granted love would make the difference, but it hadn't. He treated her and their marriage with the same indifference he did a business proposition. Once he won her over, the challenge for him was over, and she was only a prize to display.

If she lived through this, she would no longer allow herself to sit behind the television screen all day watching game shows or talk shows, stuffing her face with cookies and popcorn. Never again would she be the sitting-pretty-yes-dear type of woman. Her only fault, if it could be considered one, was in filling her life with hope and fantasy.

Then, was it so important to hold onto this kind of life? Even when it wasn't so dear after all?

She couldn't prevent her face from tightening with anger.

Because it is important, she decided.

Somehow, she was more certain now than any time ever before that it was dear to her. From this day on, if God granted her safety, she would make it so. This one, terrible episode changed her life completely. If Adam didn't like the new change, well, she'd decide what to do about it when the time came. For now, she had to get out alive. First things first.

***

How am I supposed to find her in this fucking, pitch blackness?

Emilio banged his hands on the steering wheel. Then he lunged for the glove compartment, shuffling through the contents, knocking out old maps, tissues and other small items before finding th flashlight he was looking for. Yes! He laughed out loud.

"Ha-Ha! When you put this little baby in here, darlin', you didn't think you was sealin' your doom, did ya?" he said triumphantly.

IT'S ABOUT TIME, Crater said, knowing well-enough the statement would induce anger. IF YOU'RE LUCKY, SHE MIGHT BE SITTIN' ON THE SIDE OF THE ROAD WAITIN' FOR YOU.

Emilio smacked the side of his head several times as if trying to knock Crater loose.

"I'll show you who's boss. Keep it up, Fuckhead, and see what happens!" Emilio declared. "You're gettin' to be a real pain in the ass."

He dashed out of the car and went to shine the flashlight into the woods.

It was dead.

"Damn," he screamed, and threw it to the ground with a crash. It broke into several pieces. He heard Crater chuckle. He angrily kicked the shattered pieces into the road, and stood puffing, his nostrils flaring. His gray mood darkened even more. He banged his fist into the passenger side door, leaving behind an ugly dent. Frenzied and in a deranged rage, Emilio roughly opened the car door and started throwing out tiny mementos from the dashboard. He ripped a stuffed animal to shreds. Its tiny, threaded insides flew about like floating feathers. He tore off a red bow that had been put on the dashboard, shredding it until it was nothing but a tangled mess. A holy statue was thrown to the tar-paved ground, breaking in a million pieces. He flung them in his fury, crying out in anger at the idea that he might not find her. His eyes scanned the wooded darkness.

What to do next? He couldn't possibly follow her without a

light. He'd only be running in circles. He had an idea. He went back in the car, turned it facing into the woods, and clicked on the high beams.

"It ain't over till it's over, baby," he exclaimed. The edge of the forest lit up brightly. *I'll find her now,* he thought with certainty.

SURE YOU WILL, interjected Crater. *IT AIN'T OVER TILL IT'S OVER, BRO.*

"But I stabbed her," Emilio noted out loud. "After a fall like that, she must've suffered bruises to prevent her from movin' fast."

Suddenly, his anger dissipated. He was excited by the challenge. *She's probably unconscious! Wait till she wakes up, the bitch,* he thought. *I'm gonna make her suffer for tryin' to get away from me.*

He felt the heat shoot up from his toes to his head. A wave of dizziness made him momentarily falter. He instantaneously knew it was Crater declaring his own excitement to the challenge. He started toward the woods, clenching and unclenching his fists.

"Come out, come out from wherever you are," he screamed and laughed simultaneously.

In his delirium, he momentarily hesitated.

D-Don't wanna go into the d-darkness.

He was afraid. Being afraid made him vulnerable. But Crater was there to offer him the proper dose of encouragement.

***

Victoria heard a scream of fury and a shatter of metal and glass. She spotted the car lights shining directly into the woods about thirty yards behind her and realized with certainty she had won a brief reprieve.

The night critters sounded into the night, disorienting her. They

30

seemed to surround her, enveloping her in a false, protective embrace. She could hear all kinds of sounds. Her senses seemed to have sharpened. Bushes stirred and leaves fluttered in the wind.

Although she outdistanced the reflection of light, it wasn't far enough away that the man couldn't hear her once he reached the light's end. She needed to keep moving.

Keep going, she pressed herself.

Her foot fell through a rotting tree trunk making her fall to the wooded floor. She cried out in pain as her shoulder hit the cold, hard ground beneath her, and her side pulsated in silent fury. When she stood back up, she realized she'd lost one of her Adidas sneakers, but didn't stop to look for it.

She ached all over but refused to succumb to the pain. The new-found strength within her offered a spare supply of adrenaline, and she put her best foot forward. Survival instinct and terror made her move faster. She focused ahead, and pushed harder, pumping her legs to the max. Her lungs burned in agony. A crack sounded behind her, and she froze. Slowly, she swung her head around. It was only a young raccoon scampering among the trees. Relieved, she continued wading a few steps knee-deep in high weeds. Three branches pricked her jeans, and she winced.

Although she could've sworn she heard a car drive off in the distance, she kept moving. The overused muscles in her legs and arms ached. Her mouth and throat were dry, and she licked her chapped lips. She was dehydrating rapidly. Her adrenaline level was at an all-time high, briefly blocking out the pain of her injuries, and she figured she would use it to her full advantage. She looked back only once, fearful of what she might see, but the man was not there. She lost him after all. She hoped he gave up and left. Maybe her luck had changed, but she still wasn't taking any chances.

The growth of weeds and bushes was thick, making her progress slow and difficult. She moved tediously amongst a tangle of tall grass and slipped treacherously on rocks and wet leaves. She felt like she'd been running the entire night but knew it to be only minutes. Using the additional burst of adrenaline that had been pumped into her system, she picked up her pace, sprinting faster.

Tree branches scratched her face and tugged her hair with every move. Stones and thorns pricked her feet. Scrapes and scratches adorned her arms and face, burning in exclamation. She stumbled down slopes through a tangle of knee-high weeds. Mud and wet pine needles clung to the sole of the one sneaker she had left. Her bare foot was dirt-smeared, mud caked in between her nail-polished toes. Uncovered, it was cold and numb.

Something scampered over her exposed toes, and she whimpered in fear.

She cursed her luck. On a normal day, this area would be bustling with activity, traveled by picnickers, campers and hunters on their way to a designated area of the state park. But in the middle of the night, no one had much use for the road. The surrounding wilderness was occupied only by its animal inhabitants.

It seemed she distanced herself far from the roadway. She frantically ran a zigzag, confused version of a parallel line. Because of the constant up and down ruggedness of her direction and the all-encompassing darkness, she was tricked into believing she was away from the road, when she really wasn't. The sound of an occasional passing car told her so. In truth, although she distanced herself from where she originally landed after the fall, she was still near to the roadway. She needed to be careful.

She bulled her way along a busy slope, alongside a stream. The running water gurgled beside her. A shower-splash of water could be heard up ahead. As she got closer, the sound took on the impression of a roaring waterfall. She abruptly turned to the left, not allowing herself to slow down, and ran headfirst into a boulder. She wanted to avoid falling into the water, to take a detour, but having taken the turn without thinking ahead properly, found herself dangling on the precipice of a cliff.

It happened quickly, and she couldn't stop herself in time. Suddenly, she was falling. Rocks and pebbles loosened and fell as she slipped, and they crumbled beneath her. She frantically grabbed for nearby branches, struggling for handholds or footholds, dangling momentarily until it was too late. The roughness of the bark scraped her skin as she hit tree trunks and thick branches in her descent. Then, her foot landed on empty air, and her body descended with rapid speed, gravity doing its job. The way down was a long one. The mountainside passed before her eyes in a blur. Her last thought as she glided on air was *what else can happen now?*

She crashed into the ground with extreme force. At first, the snap-crunch Victoria heard immediately made her think she broke her leg. After regaining her composure, she realized it was branches of a tree beneath her body, which cushioned her fall. The first bang to her head was bad, but this one was far worse. Thick, warm blood trickled down the back of her head and directly onto the back of her already blood drenched shirt. She lay flat on her back atop wet pine needles and fallen leaves, the sting of pain a shuddering reminder of her injuries.

The disturbing notion she might not survive this encounter after getting this far overwhelmed her. She thought of Adam.

What will he do without me? Can he survive?

She surmised he could and probably wouldn't miss her at all.

Victoria had been a shy, introverted individual for most of her life. She was no stranger to loneliness. When she met Adam, he changed this for her, making her feel loved after being neglected for so long. He catered to her every whim, sweeping her off her feet.

As she remembered it now, she wondered how she could've been such an easy target for his intentions. Was she that obvious?

Her childhood had been that of a normal, happy young girl. Although her parents weren't rich by any materialistic means, they were rich in their love for one another and for her. She grew up in a trailer park where her parents owned a two-bedroom trailer home. Her father was a laborer with a meager income, but they were happy.

When she was thirteen, her life changed dramatically when her parents died in an automobile accident. Not having any other living family, she was shuffled from one foster home to another.

One thing about her parents was they had been very smart when it came to financial matters. They set up a trust fund for her benefit in the event something bad should befall them, leaving her alone. The family lawyer was a good one, and after the liquidation of all their assets, she would receive a sum of money which would help her to an extent, but until that time she dwelled in foster care.

The sexual and physical abuse began almost immediately after being placed in the first home, and it continued regularly thereafter. It was almost as if she had a sign pasted on her forehead which read: *Abuse me – I've already been used.*

Outwardly shy and quiet, she was infinitely stronger and extroverted within. Where most children suffering from the same abusive experience would be scarred for life, Victoria was able to summon powers from within herself to help her overcome the trauma of the experiences, enabling her to suppress the abuse, to hide it, to forget the sordid details and go on with her life in the best way she knew how. As time went on, she forced herself more and more into herself, dealing with and accepting the idea of the abuse inflicted upon her as she got older and blossomed into womanhood.

After each abusive incident, she got into the obsessive habit of taking herself into the bathroom and subjecting her body to a boiling bath and body scrub down to the point at which her skin was red and raw. It was a ritual she adhered to until the abuse ceased in order to wipe away the physical impression of uncleanliness she felt was left upon her body.

During those years, she made few friends, but none of them close. She never remained in one place long enough to establish any kind of solid friendship. It wouldn't have mattered much anyway, because she lacked self-esteem. She considered herself to be used goods, not worthy of real, wholesome friendships.

When she was eighteen, she gratefully left foster care, excited to finally be able to live a normal life. She received the money from her trust fund, which wasn't very much, but it was enough to help her with college. She took a job in a McDonald's to cover her basic necessities and managed her money wisely. She started out as a cashier and worked her way up to manager, all the while attending school. Though it was a hard and lonely life to lead, she somehow always made ends meet.

She was near to reaching her teaching degree when Adam happened into the McD's for an early morning cup of coffee. The register girl failed to cap the coffee cup correctly, and it spilled onto his expensive suit. As manager, Victoria offered to replace the coffee, and pay for the cleaning bill.

One word led to another, and before she knew it, he asked her out to dinner. She could hardly believe it. She almost didn't.

She was utterly flabbergasted and thrilled by his attention. She was an easy, obvious target without even realizing it. Ten years her senior and experienced with women, Adam knew all the right moves to win her over.

Things became clearer once they were married. Adam changed. He told her only minutes into their first conversation together, he decided he would marry her. Victoria believed it was love at first sight, but Adam viewed it differently. He confessed he considered it somewhat like a business proposition. Victoria realized she had been used again, but in an entirely different manner. She resigned herself to the fact that Adam married her because it was convenient and typical of someone in his profession as CEO of Marlene Cosmetics. He needed a certain kind of wife and found it in Victoria Moor.

She accepted it as her fate in life, forever craving the initial affection her offered her so freely when they were single and unattached. Their union worked only because Victoria allowed it to. They managed to sustain a comfortable relationship, but Victoria craved love and romance, turning to books and movies to fulfill her fantasies.

Turning to Kyran Cornell.

The realization that Adam didn't really love her hit her hard and hurt tremendously. He loved the plain-Jane-ever-so-obedient wife she symbolized, and their marriage was destined to be loveless from the start.

She psychologically replaced Adam with Kyran. When fantasizing about a movie star, you could pretend they loved you however much you wanted to. She needed love, and eventually Kyran became an obsession for her.

Losing her would merely force Adam fiercely into his work. He'd probably earn a merit badge for his efforts and shoot even further up the ladder of success. He'd be fine. It was a sad realization. It was a shame he was so power-driven, because he could be a nice guy if he wanted to. Adam would never realize what he was missing, because he never truly gave it a chance, and if he ever did realize it, it'd be too late to turn back the hands of time.

Victoria suddenly came to a major decision. If she made it out alive, she'd ask Adam for a divorce. It was the right thing to do for them both. Why was she wasting valuable time worrying about him anyway? She should be thinking about getting to safety.

In a couple of hours, Adam would arrive home. Victoria wouldn't be there. She could almost hear the words of the idle conversation they would've had.

"What did you do on your night alone?" Adam would've asked.

Her response would've been, "Nothing much. I took in the latest movie starring Kyran Cornell."

***

Emilio continued the search, but to no avail. He was getting more and more pissed off by the second. Before, he was sure he'd find her. Not anymore. He was losing control of his concentration. With Crater angrily interfering, constantly putting in his two cents and the car engine rumbling, his thoughts were discombobulated.

SHE KNOWS WHAT YOU LOOK LIKE, Crater reminded him.

That's for sure. There's no way I can let her get away, Emilio thought.

He'd find her. It was only a matter of time. He was quick and clever. Experience taught him that, as the hunter, he had the advantage. He'd done it before and won. He'd do it again and win. Inexperienced, she'd eventually lose, her fear giving way to surrender. He was better at this game than she was, to say the least, but after his humiliating failure so far, he was having a hard time convincing himself of it.

He paced back and forth squinting away from the light, hoping to get a clearer view, trying to adjust his eyes to the following darkness. He reached the end of the lit area without luck. He was utterly confused.

Should I go into the darkness?

But he was afraid, and fear made him feel vulnerable.

Emilio knew this all too well. He was vulnerable in the dark, because he always was afraid of the dark.

Bad things happen in the dark.

Should I go into the dark woods without a light? he questioned himself again.

YES! YES! Crater advised insistently.

But if she reports the attack to the police and gives a description, what are the chances of them finding me?

He turned from right to left spasmodically, making lame excuses so as not to admit his fear. Back and forth continually, undecidedly.

I can't stay here all night long wasting time looking for the bitch, he reasoned.

All Emilio wanted was her car and cash. Back at the parking lot, he would've killed her right then and there. Taking her with him was Crater's bright idea. Crater wanted to toy with her. He said killing her slowly would be a thrill. Emilio knew from past experiences that Crater was right about that, but he could've done without it.

I'll leave and clear out of the area as fast as I can, he decided.

NO! NO! Crater rumbled angrily from deep within. *WANNA DO HER! WANNA RIP HER EYES OUT AFTER I USE HER.*

Emilio forcibly blocked out Crater, something which was getting harder and harder to do lately.

The sooner I hightail my ass outta here, the less chance of getting' caught, he firmly decided.

It was time he took control of things, instead of letting Crater rule the roost.

Besides, her pocketbook was in the car. It would contain identification and an address. If the need arose, he could always go back and finish her off later when the time was right. She might not even report the incident, because she was afraid of him. Or she'd tell the police she never got a look at his face.

Yeah, he decided. *It's safe to leave. I'll drive into the next town, switch the plates, and dump the car later. Who knows? She might end up dying out here on her own! No one will know anything for a very l-o-n-g time. Maybe she's already dead. I stuck her, man! She took a mean tumble!*

Crater's voice went silent, and it seemed to have finally given up.

With his decision made, his anger subsided slightly. Emilio trudged back to the car, ignoring Crater's sudden, disturbing appeal, and took off. As he clenched his fingers around the steering wheel, he cursed Hyundai for not giving the 2017 model much acceleration power.

Chapter Four

Clayton Pesce drove his blue Ford Bronco way over the speed limit. He hoped there weren't any state troopers hiding out, waiting to pull him over. The road was surrounded by a steady stretch of trees. He didn't see any spot where they could be hiding, but he was worried anyway.

He was concerned with making good time after overstaying his visit. Earlier in the evening, he packed his bag and put it in the truck, ready to leave. He'd gone back into the house to bid his farewell, when his mom convinced him to stay for dinner. She made his favorite, beef goulash, something he couldn't resist. And who in their right mind would refuse strawberry shortcake for dessert? Dinner with his parents was a five-course meal, and they could talk your ear off. Before he knew it, the time went swiftly by. But he was paying for his healthy appetite now.

Why the hell did my parents have to retire to Vernon, New Jersey of all places? Clayton was utterly perplexed. It was beyond his comprehension how anyone could be attracted to a place filled with odd names like Wawayanda Road and Breakneck Road.

When he griped about the distance and long drive, his father responded, "It's closer to civilization than Ticonderoga, New York, and not as cold. My bones're brittle, Clay. They need a rest."

Shit! That didn't make it easy for Clayton, though. Every time he paid them a yearly visit, it meant at least five hours' worth of driving, and that was without traffic. He hated it.

Since then, Clayton made sure not to mention it again. He was already on his parents' shit list. It was best to keep the peace and ensure his spot in their will, but no one would ever change his mind about his home. No matter how he looked at it, his parents' moving away from Lake George made them traitors. There was no place like it. He loved the mountains of Lake George. His tiny log cabin in the Glenburnie development of Putnam Station, New York was the top of the world. Nothing could compare. And, born and raised there, he'd remain a diehard Lake Georgian to the end. Vernon, New Jersey didn't even come close.

Clayton rummaged through the CDs on the passenger seat, scattering candy wrappers and soda cans onto the car floor, adding to the mess already accumulated there. The floor of his truck was his very own sanitation dump, littered with everything from old sneakers to orange juice containers and fast food packaging.

Clayton tried to get his mind off the long drive home. He popped in Meat Loaf's *Bat Out of Hell* and hummed along with the tunes. His favorite song, "Paradise by the Dashboard Light," was on, and it was getting him hot and bothered. Clayton knew he might have to stop the truck and hand-job himself if it really got to him. Either that or he'd have to pull over at the next truck stop and pick up a prostitute to do it for him. In a minute, he was going to have to pull over anyway, because he'd been holding a whiz in for the last ten minutes or so. Having a hard-on didn't help matters any.

He contemplated buying one of those carry-along, portable whizzers, but decided against it. Something about whipping out his Poonsie in the wide-open excited him. He felt like he was being a naughty little boy disobeying his mother. Besides, the thought of having to clean out the carry-along afterwards grossed him out.

Meat Loaf was singing his heart out. His voice was phenomenal; music to your ears. Clayton memorized the lyrics to every song. Meat Loaf's music was about the only thing that could strike a chord of emotion in him. The words were touching. Clayton thought it was amazing that such an ugly guy could write and sing so great, but people make up for things they lack in other ways.

He was glad Meat Loaf released another album after being away for so many years. He'd watched the video numerous times since then, and the man didn't look half-bad. As a matter of fact, he looked damned good. He'd even dropped a few pounds. The song, "I Would Do Anything for Love," was out of this world. He really digged the guy's stuff.

"I gotta remember to pick up that new CD," he reminded himself aloud. "I'm sure they'll still have it somewhere."

He squinted to see the road clearly through the fog. He leaned forward, pulling his sweatshirt sleeve over his hand and wiped the fogged-up windshield.

Now is as good a time as any, he decided.

He pulled off to the side of the road and clicked on the hazards.

Better to be safe than sorry, he thought.

He left the truck running and took his spare key out from under the mat. He turned the stereo up to full blast so he would be able to hear it.

Clayton liked taking a shit and piss to music. He invested in one of those shower radio jobs a while back, and stuck it to the wall next to the toilet bowl so he could flick it on whenever the need arose. After all, when doing the dude, he could be in the can for quite a while.

He leaned over to make sure he locked the passenger door. He had a fetish about locking the truck's doors and did so no matter where he was. He didn't want to give anyone the chance to steal his Baby. Even though he was on a deserted road in the middle of nowhere, he wasn't risking it.

He glanced in the rearview mirror to see if anyone was coming from behind. He looked over his yellowing teeth and smiled.

He almost never looked in a mirror, because he hardly ever brushed his teeth or hair. He didn't care much about the clothes he wore, when he wore them, or to where, but as far as some things were concerned, he was extremely particular. What did matter to him were clean towels and sheets almost every other day, his constipation and how he wiped his ass, a runny nose or sinus pain, and where he took a shit or piss.

With his short, squat physique, several chins, no neck and mop of stringy hair, Clayton Pesce resembled his idol Meat Loaf in many respects. He very easily could've been mistaken for a vagrant who hung out on street corners.

He got out of the truck and locked the door, his belly blubber falling over the rim of his waistline. He momentarily sucked in his breath, pulling the fat back inside, only to release his built-up air and have it fall over the rim again. There was too much of it to do anything about it.

He proceeded to scope out the area where he pulled over. The spot where he would relieve himself needed to be someplace comfortable. He didn't want to be taking a leak in a place that gave him the jitters. It took him a full five minutes before finally deciding on one. He released his Worshipped One to take care of business, moving rhythmically to the beat of "For Crying Out Loud" as he did so.

***

Victoria pulled herself up, using the last of her resources. Pain stabbed at her right leg, making her limp. It was swollen and tender. She caught her breath and moved onward. Each step was a sharp reminder of the fall she had taken and was made with extreme ease. The throbbing brought on sudden tears.

No. I won't give in to it, she growled.

She had come this far, why give in to it now? She reached deep within her being and grabbed hold of her inner soul, urging and finding additional strength, thinking positive. She crawled up the side of the embankment.

The rumble of a truck's engine jarred her awake. Whoever was driving it had pulled over. Victoria thought it might be to relieve themselves. Whatever the reason, she was grateful. She only had a few moments to get to the truck, and it was her only chance at getting help. The crickets continued their sounds in chorus interfering with her train of thought.

I have to get there. It's my only hope.

She was extremely sore but wasn't concerned with the possibility of doing herself any further injury. She was losing consciousness again. She lost a tremendous amount of blood, and the pain stabbing up her leg was unbearable, but she pushed forward, nonetheless.

The blue pickup, with its blinking hazards, stood alone, silently beckoning. She heard the hum of the truck's engine running. Its lights were shining ahead, and the stereo was blasted. She literally dragged herself through the bushes to get there.

When she finally reached it, panting and flushed from her efforts, she found the doors were locked.

Oh Lord! Why? Why now? She thought. *This is the boondocks! Why would they lock the doors?*

The chances of running into someone looking for trouble around here were next to nil! The chances of running into anyone at all were! People did the strangest things. If they stopped to think about it, they would've realized that encountering someone in this secluded area would've been somebody well-armed – and locked doors wouldn't make a bit of a difference – or it could've been someone in trouble. *Like me.*

She looked for any signs of the driver but couldn't see them anywhere. Darkness in the country without streetlights, and her deteriorating condition, prevented her from seeing any further than the car lights.

Victoria considered the options available to her.

Hop into the back of the truck. Don't take any chances. If she fell outside the truck, there was a chance they might not see her, and that would be the end of it. On the other hand, she barely had enough strength to get this far. If she went looking for them, and they didn't hear her calling above the radio's rumble, she could ruin her only chance.

Why the hell am I thinking about this?

They wouldn't be here for much longer

Right now, she had a chance.

One chance only.

Climb into the back, damn it!

With her last surge of energy, Victoria painstakingly lifted herself over the back into the truck. Wherever this person was going, they'd find her sooner or later. Hopefully, she'd still be alive. She fell into the back with a thud, breathing a sigh of relief above her body's cries of pain. She curled up in ball, trying to shelter herself from the cold and chill reverberating through her body.

She tried to stay conscious so she could alert them of her presence, but no sooner was her head resting on the metal floor of the pickup then her eyes began to get droopy. Her pain subsided briefly. Her body suddenly felt numb, as though it shut itself down due to power failure.

You made it, she told herself. *You're going to be fine now.*

She was pretty convincing, but she wasn't sure if she believed it or not. She struggled to keep her eyes open; her gaze lingering briefly up at the dark, vast sky. Then, they slid closed, slipping her into unconsciousness.

In a dream state, Victoria gradually fell into oblivion, down a deep well. Falling deeper into the dark chasm of blackness, she was aware of the fact she was in the world of unconsciousness but felt relaxed and comforted in its embrace. At the bottom of the shadowed well, she clearly saw Kyran Cornell smiling up at her. She wanted to go to him. Nothing else seemed important anymore.

***

Back in his bedroom in New York City, Kyran Cornell was having a fitful night of sleep. The Dream.

He whimpers.

Run. Run. Run.

A never attainable goal to reach The Woman ensues. Caught in a cold downpour, he hurries himself. He's afraid for her safety. Pursuit. The Woman's life remains unequivocally at the hands of the mysterious stranger he can't see but knows- feels with every bone in his body – is dangerous. He senses peril getting closer.

Run. Run. Run.

The threat is closer, closer. Gaining up on her.

Gaining.

He sweats and shakes uncontrollably. Soon the race will be over.

Run. Run. Run.

Before it's too late.

The thought makes Kyran even more frantic to reach her.

He pants feverishly.

Suddenly he awoke, bathed in sweat, pulse racing, lips taut with whimpers which escaped through clenched teeth, choking on fear. Confused. Glad to wake up, he folded his arms above him, cradling his head in them.

***

Dreaming allowed Victoria freedom to do whatever she pleased. And in her dream, she always wants to be with Kyran Cornell. Taking action, she swam down to his outstretched arms. Suddenly, she was entirely free of her physical self. She willed herself to remain in the dream and was momentarily disappointed that her mind disobeyed. She saw her body below her lying in the back of the pickup and was disgusted at the sight of her condition.

I must be dead, she thought. *Otherwise, what could be happening?*

She didn't understand. Had she forgotten?

I'm outside my body. Maybe I'm dying. Or maybe I'm dead and I'm a ghost.

No.

She realized she wasn't, because her chest was moving vividly up and down in slow, steady motion.

She remembered.

All of it came back to her in a whoosh. She was having an out-of-body experience.

During her teen years, she read up on it after having similar experiences during the molestation period of her childhood. Back then, she drew herself outward into another room of the house where she created a world of make-believe where everything was wonderful – where she was happy. By doing this, she'd been able to relieve herself of the pain inflicted by the traumatic violations. She never felt what happened to her, merely the aftereffects. She discovered the similarities of her experience with those of others depicted in a television program, and she went to the library to do some research. She was never certain the out-of-body theory applied to her, but then the explanation seemed plausible. Having an explanation eased the hidden notion she might be psychologically ill.

Now, although the circumstances differed, she was involved in an extremely traumatic situation. It wasn't hard for her to make the connection between what happened to her many years before with what was happening to her now. Since that time in her life, she carefully kept her distance in avoiding pressured, difficult incidents. Nothing had yet happened to totally throw her mind into a fear so great she would want to leave.

Until now.

The attack and abduction had been too much. Her astral body was apparently attempting a voyage.

She concentrated and willed herself back inside her body only to find herself in darkness.

No.

She didn't want to be in the darkness. She wanted The Dream. She wanted Kyran.

Up and down she frantically worked but found no way out.

Forward. Backward. Right. Left.

Darkness. Closing in fast around her.

So quickly. Quicker. No way out.

Silently screaming, she was unable to open her eyes or move her limbs but knew for certain she had reentered her physical self. She became frightened. No matter how much she tried, she could neither escape the darkness nor bring the Kyran dream back.

With every possible effort, she concentrated on the task at hand. She knew there she would be safe.

***

Driving steadily on Interstate 17, Clayton noticed the clouds moving in fast, but the wind finally abated. If it continued to rain, it would slow him down considerably, ruining any time he might've made since starting out, and he was eager to reach his home territory.

As he drove along, he sang along with Meat Loaf. The words, "Can't you see my faded Levi's burstin' apart," sent spasms through his loins. He was heartily looking forward to getting back home, but his thoughts of the present were of a far different nature. As The Worshipped One grew in reaction to the song's words, Clayton thought, *I may have to pull over at the truck stop after all.*

A blowjob suddenly became first priority.

***

Emilio kept off the county roads and highways, remaining on unmarked roads. He didn't know where he was going, only that he had to keep moving, never staying in one place long enough to be noticed.

After driving around a dinky town called Layton for what seemed like an eternity, he finally found the perfect spot, set up the scene to look as though he had car trouble, and waited for a sucker to drive by.

It wasn't long before the proud owner of a Chevy shitbox pulled over to offer assistance. The guy was in his late seventies, thin, short, weak looking, wearing construction boots, brown polyester pants and a blue flannel shirt over his windbreaker. He stood for a moment at the rear of the Hyundai, assessing the situation. Then, he walked over to Emilio.

As the man walked toward him, Emilio moved so quickly the man never saw it coming. Small and fragile, the man was nowhere near a match to Emilio's bulk. The old man's shocked expression invigorated Emilio. The Need gave him strength. He whipped out his blade shouting immediate orders from which the old man cringed but obeyed.

The smell of blood seeped far back in his nostrils, urging and compelling him to take advantage of the situation.

He made the Bozo pull up ahead of the Hyundai. Then, he forced the old bugger out of the car to watch while he set the Hyundai afire. The old man tried to run, but Emilio restrained him. This merely enraged and excited Emilio further.

The Hyundai was a fiery heap. Metal, upholstery, and plastic melting in the night. The devouring flames roared like fireballs. Before long, it would be nothing but charred remains.

Amidst the orangey, hot flames he slit the man's throat, flesh parted, and the blood flowed freely. It was over in a matter of seconds, but the thrill was enough to last a lifetime. As Emilio watched the blood flow in spurts, jerky spasms or orgasm ripped through his loins making him lose control. A gooey wet patch decorated the front of his jeans.

His Need was satisfied for the moment. The Need was so intense at times and induced by a hatred so great, but Emilio rationalized it as part of his revelation, his fate.

This was something he was so absolutely convinced of without question. Committing slaughter soothed the aching need for fulfilling his revelation. And each time he killed he was one step closer to heaven.

One step closer to his divine proclamation and total fulfillment of his destiny.

He left the old guy's body alongside the burning car and traded the bitch's car in for the Chevy bombshell.

Beggars can't be choosers.

It was the only thing that happened along. The disadvantage of driving a stolen car is that you couldn't rely on its operation. Luckily, the keys were in the ignition. The car stuttered but moved. Emilio only hoped it would get him as far as the next town.

He glanced at the passenger seat and saw a brown paper bag of groceries. Where the old geezer was shopping at this hour of the night baffled him, but he was glad, nonetheless.

They'll come in handy, he thought to himself.

Emilio dug into the bag, pulling out a six pack of Pepsi, a hero sandwich, a container of coleslaw, and two Mars candy bars.

The old bugger had a pretty hardy appetite for his puny physique, Emilio gratefully admonished.

He wouldn't have stopped for food for the next couple of hours at least. One less thing to worry about. On the interstate again, steadily doing seventy miles per hour, he grabbed one of the cans of soda, tugging it off its plastic ring overwrap. He popped it open, taking a long swig, then braced it between his legs while driving. He noticed the tank was almost on empty and decided to stop to refill the gas and use the restroom.

Life is so wonderful, he thought to himself.

MURDER IS MORE FUN, Crater exclaimed from within. Emilio had to agree.

Chapter Five

It was turning out to be an overly long drive for Clayton. Even stopping for a rendezvous hadn't been enough to lift his spirits. It was short-lived and expensive. The girl probably sensed his anxiousness. Either that, or The Worshipped One's abnormally large size gave it away. The chick wasn't even a looker. He'd stopped twice more along the way to piss again, which was a chore, and he got the munchies along the way.

He allowed himself to give into his junk food desire only once when he saw a clean, well-stocked twenty-four hour store in Albany. Then, he picked up Cheese Doodles, Herr's Honey Mustard Pretzels, a Dove Bar, two ice cream sandwiches- which he ate immediately before they melted- and two Cokes. He wasted an enormous amount of time mulling over the selection in the display case. Like a young boy whose eyes were bigger than his stomach – at least they were at one time in his life – he couldn't decide what he wanted and how many of it. Finally, he'd made his decisions, and was sorry for not grabbing MalloCups while he was at it.

Now, as he was winding on the last stretch homeward bound, his stomach unbelievably cried out for scrambled eggs and corned beef hash.

Lake Champlain filled the large expanse on his right. He unconsciously scanned it surface in search of its famed monster to catch a glimpse and be one among the select few who already had. He drove into the early morning sunshine, which according to the weatherman, would be short-lived before rain started up again. He wasn't bothered by this. He immediately relaxed. He was home and in his own familiar territory.

He looked down at the dash clock. It was going on 5 AM. He

remembered his fridge was empty. He'd cleaned it out before taking his trip. He hadn't wanted to arrive home to a refrigerator that stunk like the garbage due to spoiled milk, rotten eggs and last month's tuna.

He wasn't in the mood to prepare breakfast for himself either. That meant having to stop and pick up the groceries first, which would take him a good two hours minimum. Whenever he shopped at the market, he fussed over every selection and came home with more than he bargained for. Plus, he never went food shopping without his coupons. They were *money*. Not using them would be like throwing away quarters and dimes which, in the end, always added up.

The cashier girls ran for the hills when they saw Clayton coming. They knew they'd be punching in coupons till doomsday. Clayton saved himself $30 alone on coupons a couple of times. Of course, he had a lot of groceries, too, but $30 was still $30.

No. There was no way he was going grocery shopping now.

He thought of The Fone Booth Diner in Middlebury, Vermont, just over the border, not even fifteen minutes from home. He decided he liked the idea of sitting down to a good home-cooked breakfast with Peggy, the regular waitress there, to serve him. She had tits the size of basketballs, and when she leaned over...

With his decision made, Clayton made the appropriate turn, and headed in the direction of The Fone Booth Diner.

***

It was hours later when Victoria awoke to a blurry world in the back of the pickup. Regaining consciousness, she realized the truck was moving. Although the bed was roomy, a metal object dug into the small of her back causing additional pain. She was no longer surrounded by a forest in darkness. The early morning sunlight was a welcome relief, warming her aching body, but stinging her eyes.

She tried to lift her head but was too dizzy. As her sight slowly cleared, the blue clouds above swerved and swirled. A passing bird soaring overhead appeared to be doing an awkward version of a breakdance. She heard an airplane in the far distance.

Victoria touched her hand to her head and felt dried, caked blood stuck to her hair. It was on her shirt and pant leg, as well. She lost a lot of blood. Her stomach cried out with hunger pangs. Her clothing was still damp from the previous night's rainfall.

Where am I, and what happened to me? She questioned herself, momentarily disoriented.

The rumble of blasted rock music could be both felt and heard coming from the cab of the truck. The Boom-Boom-Boom of the drums reverberated underneath her. She could tell they were moving, and it made her even more nauseous.

She turned over and groaned in protest. Her breathing was raspy and hard, and her chest ached. A heating sensation emanated from within her body. She lifted herself onto her hands and immediately became winded. Her eyes just made it over the side of the truck. She was able to hold on for only a few short seconds before falling back down again, reawakening the pain in full force. She managed to hold on long enough to catch sight of a rest stop with public facilities and a road sign that read Middlebury, Vermont. She mumbled the name out loud. She watched as a single leaf fluttered and soared above her, floating on a gentle breeze in the empty blue-gray sky.

"Kyran!" she called, barely a whisper, before blacking out for good. Back in the world of darkness, Victoria concentrated hard on leaving her body again, remembering how she did it so many years before. She relaxed her mind and body, breathing rhythmically. She unconsciously honed in on her focus and felt her body become rigid as her spirit body separated from the physical one, leaving an empty shell behind. Gradually, she extended her focus point.

Six feet. Above the truck.

Then, twelve feet above the roadway.

She clearly saw the truck driving steadily down the paved highway, slowly disappearing around a bend and out of sight.

She concentrated on maintaining full control of her abilities and propelled herself toward the point of destination. Suddenly finding herself in a state of joy and ecstasy, her astral body continued to rise. Trees, water and wildlife filled the large expanse beneath her. Before long, she was enveloped in cottony, white clouds.

If she couldn't have Kyran in her dream world, she'd go to him in the only reality she now had access to. She wished herself in New York City and the apartment building where she'd seen him photographed so many times in various magazines. In her mind, she clearly depicted its surroundings and floated in that direction. She felt as though she were moving faster than the speed of light, but even that wasn't fast enough.

***

In his Manhattan apartment, Kyran awoke in a sweat, guessing the hour to be sometime early morning. It was almost light out. He was tossing fitfully in the middle of The Dream in its new version, when terror drew him outward. Even though he knew he was awake and in his own bedroom, he couldn't shake the terror scene of The Dream away.

He turned and rolled over, punching his pillow in an attempt to fluff it up some, and ended up staring blankly at the white, stucco ceiling.

He was confused.

The last couple of nights he had only brief snatches of sleep, coming fully awake at the point in The Dream when he'd come near to reaching The Woman, and she'd disappear. Then, his frantic search to locate her would ensue.

He was going completely crazy. He couldn't eat, sleep or think properly. The Woman and The Dream became more demanding and desperate in their nature. Kyran was convinced he was at the breaking point, losing his mind. He'd succumbed to taking sleeping pills, something he never did before, in the hopes it would help him get rest. He had no other choice. The sleeplessness and anxiety reached the point where it was interfering with his work.

Just yesterday afternoon, while doing a take of his new movie, *Margarita*, Kyran had a screaming match with Julia on the set, and this annoyed him. Since their one night together, she developed an emotional attachment to him, even though he warned her against it. Since then, she took to calling him regularly and coincidentally showing up wherever he went. She constantly dropped in on the set, disrupting the entire crew. Julia was overly persistent, angering Kyran to the point where he snapped.

Julia created yet another stir when she ran off crying. Even though she provoked the incident by grabbing for his privates in front of the crew, it was unnecessary for him to react as he had. Normally, he would've pushed her hand away and pulled her over to the side to privately speak with her. He was definitely losing control.

The sleeping pills weren't very effective. They merely made him toss into a sleep so deep he had a hard time rousing himself from the nightmare of The Dream.

His nerves were close to snapping. He tried rationalizing the situation. He never had a 'crazy day' in his life. Never once did he 'lose it'. Therefore, The Woman had to be real. She *had* to exist. Otherwise, he would need to accept the possibility he was mentally disturbed and in need of psychiatric help. Rationalizing gave him a will to survive and overcome whatever it was that ailed him. She *was* real. He resigned himself to that fact to save his sanity. All he needed to do was find her.

But how?

Oh God! I need to find her. Help me find her in time.

He was fearful The Woman was suffering from some terribly final crisis, and he couldn't do a damn thing about it. He felt he had a special obligation to her. Some might have disagreed with his reasoning, but he felt a strong commitment to her. Finding and helping her were the most important things in his life. He needed that desperately.

He lost his mom when he was four. He was turned over to his grandmother's care, because his father, a working actor, was gone much of the time. Although he and his father had a very close relationship, it was hard to uphold. Show business didn't leave much room for family life. His father did the best he could, but the bonding Kyran craved was always far out of reach.

Just when he started to feel close to his grandmother, she passed away. From then on, it was nannies all the way through his teens, and the close-knit bonding he craved was lost forever.

To date, he and his father were still close. They made up as much as they could for the lost time, but Kyran's childhood memories were a thing of the past and couldn't be brought back no matter how hard they tried. He still craved something real and solid, something he could build upon right from the start.

He wanted a real home. One where, if necessary, it must be guarded or distanced from the rest of the world or protection's sake. One where he'd go home and still have a whole family.

As for The Woman, she was kind of a symbol for what he wanted, as though the fate of his destiny lay in her survival. He knew with the utmost certainty that, if it came down to it, he'd even die for The Woman if he needed to and make the extreme sacrifice so she could go on living. It'd be worth the effort, knowing he fulfilled a purpose in life at the end. But, if he found her and saved them both, he'd do it without a second thought. The whole thing felt like he was playing a part in one of his movies.

He rubbed his weary eyes, pondering the idea of getting up for a cold glass of water. His throat was dry and parched. He closed his eyes, trying to relax.

A thump-thumping sound at the window alarmed him and was afraid to open his eyes to look. The thump-thumping sound continued.

Thump-Thump-Thump-Thump.

It's nothing.

Thump-Thump.

Don't bother looking. He breathed in deeply, willing the noise to stop. Now his nerves were frayed.

Thump-Thump.

The noise began to irritate him.

When he finally forced himself to look over at the window, he saw it was a loose cable wire flapping against the window, hitting the glass like a giant, mutant black snake attempting to gain entrance to feed on its unwilling prey within. He would need to remember to call the cable company to come in and take care of the problem.

Growing outside winds voiced their presence.

Nothing strange. Nothing to get so weirded-up about.

Yet, he still couldn't shake the nervous energy which forced him awake in the first place. He lay there trembling. His hands started shaking uncontrollably as he attempted to pull his satin comforter up against his chest. He knew he was treading on the edge of paranoia, slowly losing control. He closed his eyes again, trying to replay the final moments of The Dream, but couldn't summon them up. He decided to urge his body up and into the bathroom for that glass of water. He slowly opened his eyes, glancing around at his satin-infested bedroom – his last short-lived conquest's idea – and finally swung his feet out of bed, tossing the comforter disgustedly aside.

I need to get rid of this crap and switch over to good old cotton, he thought.

The sound of his telephone ringing startled him yet again. He stopped dead in his tracks.

Who the hell would be calling at this crazy hour?

He decided to let the answering machine pick up.

What if it was some sort of emergency?

He was just about to run for it when the machine clicked on.

Might as well find out who it is first.

Julia Beckett's voice came on the line repeating his thoughts exactly.

"My goodness, Kyran. Where could you be at this ungodly hour? I was calling to apologize for the way I acted to you this afternoon. I hope you haven't gone out to find somebody new already. I'd be extremely disappointed."

Apologizing? At this hour? Definitely not, he thought. *She's got an underlying factor for calling for sure. She's a very persistent girl who's probably temporarily lonely, couldn't sleep, and wants attention. Spoiled brat! How could I have been so stupid to get involved with her? What was I thinking? Just what I need right now. Correction. Just what I don't need.*

He let her talk until she finally hung up. Knowing Julia, she wouldn't remain lonely for long. She'd find someone willing enough to soften her mood no matter what time it was.

Shuffling his way into the bathroom, he turned on the faucet, letting the water run full blast. The bathroom wood-framed mirror was dirty, but clearly reflected Kyran's facial expression and mood. He sighed and haphazardly took the water glass off the sink when, at the edge of his vision, he caught sight of a shadow and was suddenly paralyzed with fear.

What the fuck, he thought.

He dropped the glass onto the floor, shattering it to pieces. Still, he didn't turn to look. Kyran gulped bile. He forced his eyes to look in the direction of the apparition. It was The Woman. He slapped his face, as if to awaken himself.

This is ridiculous, he thought. *Now I'm dreaming The Dream while I'm fully awake!*

He put his hand on the doorframe to steady himself, leaning against it momentarily, catching his forehead in his hand.

What's happening to me?

She seemed perfectly solid, not at all transparent, as she stood blocking the closet doorway directly beside the bed. Her body appeared weightless. She remained that way with a sad look in her eyes.

He slowly walked over to her and cautiously put out his hand to touch her, but his hand fell through open air. He took a step back, convinced she was a vision of his imagination. Then she spoke.

"Middlebury, Vermont."

Kyran could neither move nor speak. He immediately collapsed onto the bed and called out, "Who are you?"

"Kyran!" she cried, her voice sounding frail, and then vanished as quickly as she had appeared.

Am I going nutso? No. There's no way in hell I could be that crazy!

The impression that mind-to-mind communication was occurring was so strong he didn't question it or hesitate a moment longer. He needed to get to Middlebury, Vermont as quickly as possible. Somehow, through their bizarre spiritual connection, a telepathic cry for help surged through.

The premonition of death made him shake uncontrollably. For all he knew, she might already be dead and this call for help a delayed reaction.

He needed to find out.

He jumped into the shower without waiting for the water to heat up. The icy water woke him completely for the time being. He needed to arouse his senses for what was in store. He got the distinct impression he was entering into something so totally strange he hoped he would have the courage to confront it all. At half past six, after making quick reservations at The Middlebury Inn, Kyran was headed on his way. He settled down to thoughts of chivalry and heroism and hoped for the best.

Hoped to find The Woman in time.

Just hoped.

Maybe his luck would change.

It had to change.

He left his apartment with high hopes.

***

Within minutes, Clayton anxiously reached his destination. The Fone Booth Diner was situated on a dead-end street directly across from a Gaseteria. An odd place for both types of businesses to be located, but Clayton was aware of the fact the Gaseteria doubled as a bookie joint. It brought in good business for the diner with the constant traffic of betters and losers.

He parked his truck in the small lot adjacent to the diner and slid over to the passenger side door, shuffling the empty Dove Bar wrapper, Cheese Doodle and pretzel bags and two empty Coke bottles. In order to reach the door lock and make sure it was pressed closed. He went directly inside.

He took the corner booth in Peggy's work area, slid way in close to the window, and waited for her to bring the menu. The corner booth table was long and wide, usually pre-set for a family of four to six, but seeing the place was near to empty at that early hour, he didn't think it made a difference. Besides, sitting at that table gave him the advantage he needed.

Out of the corner of his eye, he glimpsed Peggy sauntering his way, and quickly spat on the opposite side of the table as far as he could reach. He managed to finish his task without being discovered milliseconds before she reached him.

"Mornin' Clayton," she said.

"Mornin' Peg," he responded, eyeing the spittle in disgust. "Never ceases to amaze me how people can go and do such a gross, unmannerly thing like that."

She responded, open-mouthed and wide-eyed, "There ain't been nobody settin' here yet this mornin'. I can't imagine who coulda done it."

The look on her face was one of dismay and confusion.

"Gimme a sec, and I'll clear that up for ya'. I 'pologize fer the mess, Clay. Ya know I'da never left it there had I'da knowed 'bout it."

Peggy was a tall woman with red hair styled in the beehive look of the sixties. Outside of work, if anyone were ever fortunate enough to see her then, she dressed the same sixties way, as if she didn't want to let go of her youth. Clayton ran into her a couple of times at the local Walmart. Once, she was wearing a short skort and tye-dye tank top. He followed her around the store until she caught sight of him. For her age, she was still in fairly good shape, buxom and big-butted. Lines furrowing around the corners of her eyes were the only sign likely to give her age away.

"Not a problem," Clayton said, smirking as he watched her rush off to get a washcloth. *She's a little ditsy upstairs, but that don't matter none,* he thought. *Yessiree, eating breakfast is going to be a pleasure for sure, a mighty good start to a new day.* He took a deep breath, releasing it gently.

He looked around at the imaginative décor of the place; its oddity and creativeness. Each time he saw it, it excited him almost as much as Peggy did.

Almost. Not quite.

The owner installed genuine telephone poles throughout the inside perimeter. Telephone lines were connected from pole to pole as if they were connecting functioning lines. Huge white streetlamps hung from each pole, but instead of illuminating roads below, they lit up the table and booth area underneath. Along every available wall were dozens of shelves displaying telephones from every era in time since its invention.

Neat idea. Fone Booth. Even the incorrect spelling is creative. Catchy. It sticks in the mind.

Clayton really liked eating here.

Peggy returned and diligently cleared up the gooey mess, leaning over much to Clayton's enjoyment. Although short-lived, it was enough to make The Worshipped One announce his approval. Peggy had a nice ass.

She took Clayton's double order of scrambled eggs and corned beef hash, toast and coffee, and left him to wallow in his dream fantasy of her.

***

Kyran travelled for five hours straight. His eyes were grainy and bloodshot. His exhaustive state made him totally unprepared for this lengthy drive, but he didn't have much further to go. To the right of the highway, a road sign indicated he'd soon reach the town of Middlebury, Vermont. He intently watched the road ahead, occasionally surveying and scanning the surrounding mountainside to look for landmarks and side road markings.

He was afraid for The Woman whose destiny lay in the hands of the stranger stalking her. There was always the chance that Middlebury would prove to be a dead end. If not, when he got there, he might find she was already dead. He might never have the opportunity to express his feelings, or kiss and hold her in reality, rather than just in The Dream.

He unconsciously pushed his foot down on the accelerator, desperate to reach his destination as quickly as possible.

Once he arrived in Middlebury, he'd check in at the Middlebury Bed & Breakfast and immediately head over to the station house thereafter. He wasn't certain whether it would get him anywhere, but it was worth the try. At this point in time, the station house and the hospital were the only two options he could think of to check out first.

The drive was taking an ominously long amount of time. Kyran knew as soon as he arrived in Middlebury, he'd be anxious and agitated for action, and would most certainly be trying his patience. The situation called for the necessity of it. If he slipped one iota, he was he going to appear to the law-abiding citizens of Middlebury? A deranged movie actor seeking a missing woman in danger whose name he didn't even know. Whose existence he wasn't even certain of but for nightmares in which she cries out "Middlebury, Vermont" in exasperated anguish? He definitely couldn't tell them the truth. He realized he'd have to take caution in his explanation and make up a story which would sound logical enough, but not the least bit suspicious.

As he made the final turn off of Interstate 95 at the Harmonyville exit, he was already scheming and devising a plan. He felt frightened, excited and warm inside all at the same time, because he understood he was so very close. For all he knew, in a matter of hours, he might be in the company of the mysterious Woman of his dreams, and he had no idea what those circumstances might entail.

Even the beautiful intermixing voices of Elton John and Kikki Dee in a love song coming through his car stereo couldn't shake the nervous tension he was feeling inside.

"If you can hear me," he spoke out loud, "I want you to know I'm coming. I'm on my way, and I'll be there as soon as I can."

***

Although his breakfast was a huge and hardy one, Clayton was almost tempted to order another portion. He had an unquenchable hunger that wouldn't cease but decided against it. Later in the evening, he'd have to do the food shopping anyway to stock up the fridge after being gone for two whole weeks. There was no way he could survive the night with an empty fridge.

"Will you be havin' anythin' else this mornin', Clay?" Peggy asked.

The expression on her face made it clear she was hoping he'd say no. She mumbled to herself and gave him a stiff smile.

"No, darlin'. That'll be all for today," he responded, and smiled back like Dopey, one of Snow White's seven dwarf friends. "You can write me up the check."

Peggy wrote it up right then and there, ripped it off the pad, and dropped it on the table in front of Clayton.

"Nice day to ya, Clay," she said, and walked off without awaiting a response.

Clayton picked it up and looked it over. Eight and change.

Eating out costs a bundle these days, he thought, even if it *was* a double order.

With difficulty, he dug his chubby fingers into his pocket. His stomach was bloated after eating so much; triple its normal size. He pulled out a five-dollar bill and four singles, quickly dropping them on the tabletop. He lazily lifted himself out of the booth.

Man-oh-man do I ever have to take a mean shit, he exclaimed to himself. *And there ain't no way I'm usin' the toilet in this joint.*

He'd have to hold it in until he got home, which wouldn't be very long, but for him it would be long enough.

He clambered out and away from the Fone Booth Diner. The morning sun did nothing to lighten the chill of the morning air, sending goosebumps along his body. It only made the necessity of his present need more demanding of his attention. He was stuffed, his stomach ached from the abundance of food, and his ass hurt from the load of shit crying to be released. He looked up at the pale Vermont sky as if in search of godly aid.

He quickly glanced at his watch. It was a little after six AM. So much for regularity! Normally, he'd do his dude at seven-thirty AM like clockwork, but the crazy length of the trip, his midnight snacking binge, and the way-too-early breakfast totally threw him off course. He was tempted to try to hold it in until the said time in order to get back on his *regular* schedule, but his mom always told him *holding it in* was unhealthy. He was damned either way, though, because if he didn't hold it in his system would remain off course, and he'd have a bout of constipation or diarrhea to fend with the next couple of days. He wasn't accustomed to irregularity.

The town was already alive with the early risers of its population. Clayton breathed in a strong gust of air, releasing a cold, plumed and frosty response. As he approached the rear of his pickup, he busily concentrated on holding *it* in.

At least hold it in until you get home, he summoned himself, squeezing his buttock cheeks tightly together and waddling along.

He almost reached the back end of the truck when he noticed something lying in a heap in the back compartment. He wasn't immediately alerted to it because of his deep-set concentration on his crying bodily needs.

"What the h—" he exclaimed. He knew the rear was empty, containing only his single suitcase and a few loose tools. Now there appeared to be something long and large lying in a tumble. And, as he drew closer, realization informed him it wasn't some*thing*, but some*body*. A woman to be exact. By the way she was positioned, with her arm thrown above her and her head lolling oddly, she looked to be in bad shape.

"Holy shit!"

His needs were all but forgotten. The sight of her filled Clayton with odd pangs of compassion, something out of the ordinary for his normally self-centered persona.

He bolted in the truck's direction and leaned over the side, numbly sticking out his shaking finger and searching for a throbbing pulse. It was faint, but it was there.

"Hold on, little lady," he said to her, knowing full-well she probably couldn't hear him. "I'm goin' to get you some help straight away!"

Forgetting his need to crap, he headed shakily back toward the entrance of the diner, breaking into a run, which for Clayton was a fast walk. He passed by a pay phone on the wall outside the diner.

It'll be quicker to use the phone inside, he reasoned. *Besides, it'll save me the quarter, and maybe win me some brownie points with Peggy.*

Peggy and the diner's chef Charlie looked disgruntled as Clayton reentered the front double doors. Their faces soon developed stunned expressions as they noticed the anxious reddened and bedraggled look on Clayton's face. He was gasping for breaths of air in between his gust of words, "Needtouse-breath-thephone-breath-emergency!"

"What in God's name is the problem with you, Clay?" Peggy hammered out, eyeing Charlie with a questioning glance. She rolled her eyes and sucked in her breath awaiting his response.

"Ladyinbackofmytruck..." He struggled to get the words out.

"So," Charlie responded and laughed, "Jest ask her to get outta the truck."

He continued to chuckle.

"Calm down, Clay," Peggy interjected. "Catch yer breath and tell us what yer talkin' 'bout."

Clayton breathed several times, making a show of his efforts.

"I went out-breath-to my truck," he said while sucking in deep breaths, "and there was this lady-breath-out cold in the back."

Realizing he finally got their full attention and relishing every moment of it, he continued.

"She's got dried blood all over her-breath-and I think she's near dead."

"My God, man," Charlie shouted. "Why in the hell didn' ya' say that in the first place?"

Charlie ran for the phone and dialed nine-one-one. Peggy ran for the door. Summoning up a second wind, Clayton darted ahead of her and was first out the door. He didn't want anybody else taking the credit for his heroism. When he reached the woman, she was in the same position she had been in when he left her. Aside from being bloodied, she looked extremely cold. Clayton felt his stomach churn with cramps of indigestion, and he thought how the makers of Mylanta would be getting rich on him alone. He tried convincing himself it wasn't nerves, but what he ate during the last couple of hours, but he knew this wasn't the case.

"Don't jest stand there," Peggy hollered from behind him. "Do something!"

Her expression revealed obvious disapproval, setting Clayton into motion again. He wrapped and old, dirty drop cloth around the woman to keep her warm. She felt cold to the touch.

"Don't be a fool, Clay," Peggy hollered. "That ain't goin' to be enough. Take of yer jacket and wrap that 'round her, too. She'll catch her death of cold if she hasn't already."

He turned around, eyeing Peggy half-wittedly.

"Go on," she instructed, shooing him with her hand.

He hesitantly obeyed her instructions. While he did so, he

realized it'd be no time at all before he'd be back on his regular shitting schedule. He had no *choice* but to *hold it in* whether his mother believed it was an unhealthy thing to do or not. Clayton was suddenly freezing cold without his fur-lined jacket. Yet another problem to fend with.

***

The lack of healthy sleep took a toll on Kyran, and the long drive was only making it worse. He took several wrong turns on the way. It was noontime, lunchtime, and his stomach didn't hesitate to remind him. All though he had grabbed fruit, chocolate covered donuts and Fage from his fridge when leaving earlier that morning, his stomach was crying out in sharp pangs.

Nevertheless, he'd first check into his room and then pursue information on The Woman without stopping to rest. He simply had to find some time in between to grab something to relieve the hunger pains. Although he was overtired, he knew he'd be unable to sleep. He couldn't afford to waste any time.

The streets were bustling with movement. A car horn blared, an out-of-towner according to the plates, and people shuffled about avoiding collisions with one another. Although there was major congestion going on, everyone appeared to be courteous to one another. No one seemed incensed or aggravated. Kyran noticed there weren't any stop signs or traffic lights in town directing cars, but they stopped to let pedestrians cross at each intersection anyway. It seemed to be common knowledge and courtesy; a quaint and organized structure.

It'd be a relief to be away from New York for a while. New York certainly had appeal with its theater district, sky-rise buildings and free shows put out by struggling musicians and comedians in Central Park, but it also included punkheads, skinheads, bums, druggies, muggers, perverts, transvestites and the homeless, just to name a few, all of which Kyran could do without. He drove along with the flow. The town was small which meant finding The Woman shouldn't be very hard at all.

He winced as images of the blood laden Woman of The Dream flashed at him. It shook him so terribly he dared not think of it further. If he allowed it to get the best of him, he'd lose all control and go mad. He instantly dismissed it from his mind and concentrated on locating the inn. The woman on the phone instructed him it was five blocks in on Main Street as soon as you entered the town limits. He started counting the intersections as he passed them.

The town was simple; Victorian. There wasn't any sign of new construction whatsoever. Every structure, though well-maintained, was old and dated from the 1700s and 1800s according to numbers displayed atop the structures to indicate the date of its completion. 1801. 1825. 1754. The entire town was a hue of pastel colors. Kyran instantly liked it there, and his mood softened. He thought it was storybook wonderful, and not for a minute did he miss the rush-hour, 24-hour days he lived with in Manhattan. He was happy not to have to deal with the hustle and bustle that went along with the territory. New Yorker etiquette left a lot to be desired. He wouldn't for a minute miss he muggers, crazy taxi drivers or drug-crazed bums.

He relaxed a little bit, breathing in deeply, allowing the air out slowly to help him relax further. His heart suddenly stopped racing.

After parking the car in the inn's small lot, Kyran went in through an entrance door which was small in physical stature and laden with hundreds of nails driven about, a definitive sign of prestige and wealth in the olden days. An enormous beam of oak whose original purpose was to bolt the door was now fastened down and used as a mere decoration. He walked into the reception area where he found an oversized woman behind the reception desk.

She was roly-poly, both her head and face the perfect shape of a circle. Gray hair fashioned in a feminine bun donned the top of her head. Hers was a friendly face. On first glance, Kyran thought he might be looking at Mrs. Santa Claus herself.

Rose-colored cheeks dotted the side of her face and appeared almost to be protruding from her cheekbones. Her chubby hands were folded in front of her on the counter. She stood erect with a smile painted on wide. Her flower-printed housedress screamed out in color, as if she hadn't a care in the world but to stand and await the arrival of her newest boarder. Enormous breasts swelled and receded with each silent, steady breath.

He glanced around at the surroundings. The inn was quaint, simple and comfortable as was the town of Middlebury itself.

A lovely, wide stairwell led up to the rooms on the second and third floor, decorated by a winding, wood-crafted banister. Beautiful paintings of different outdoor scenes adorned the wallpapered walls on all sides. There were tree-lined lake views, water views with steamships rolling, ocean views with waves roaring underneath a bright-colored sunset. Each one created a different mood so realistic one could close their eyes and picture themselves in the midst of it all.

Kyran became engrossed in one depicting snow-covered mountain peaks. In it, he pictured a log cabin where he and The Woman lay on a down comforter together by a warm fire touching softly, talking quietly. He was so involved in his daydream he almost didn't hear when the woman behind the counter spoke.

"May I help you, sir?" she asked in a dry, but friendly Vermont accent.

"Oh, Y-Yes," Kyran answered, embarrassed at being caught in a daze. "My name is Cornell. I have a reservation."

"Cornell what?" she asked politely.

"Oh, I'm sorry," he said. "Kyran Cornell."

"Oh, yes. Of course," she replied. "I'm terribly sorry. I should've recognized you. It isn't often we have a celebrity among us. If you'll just sign here in the ledger, please."

She pointed to a blank line and handed him a pen.

"Your room is nine."

She rang a silver bell atop the desk.

"I'll have someone show you to your room. I hope you enjoy your stay here, and if there's anything you need, be sure to let me know."

"Thank you," Kyran said, as a young, teenage boy ran up beside him.

"Yes, Mrs. Grabowski?" the boy asked, looking at the woman while darting his eyes sideways at Kyran. He obviously recognized Kyran and appeared a bit nervous.

"Josh, dear," she said. "Would you please be kind enough to show Mr. Cornell to his room?"

Nothing like good ol' Vermont hospitality.

"I certainly will, ma'am," he answered in the same dry, polite droll, as he took the key from Mrs. Grabowski's outstretched hand.

He was a young kid. About sixteen. He was wearing a baseball cap on backwards and jeans that sagged in the ass, making it appear like he had no ass to fill it. The pants appeared to be a few sizes too big. His attire was definitely not New York Plaza, but Kyran gratefully accepted the fact, and preferred the common Middlebury politeness to the New York attitude anyway. Besides, all clothing oversized was the *in thing* nowadays. Little kids were wearing shirts two sizes larger, high top sneakers untied with the tongues hanging up and walking with a bop that showed they had *personality.* Teens were wearing their jeans two and three sizes too big, hanging down with their boxers showing.

Kyran followed Josh up to his room. As they walked straight ahead, Kyran looked into French doors which led into a dining area which may have been used as a parlor in a long-ago time. Kyran stopped briefly to admire it.

A fireplace was on the wall with an aged wood mantelpiece adorned with antiques from centuries past: a rusted scale, a water jug, and an etched plate on a stand. Leaning up against the wall directly beside it stood a stained-glass window, probably once belonging to a church, with a few of its colored panes cracked from age.

Heavy brocaded, red curtains hung from long, colonial windows. Table napkins of the same bright shade decorated the tabletops at each place setting. Someone eating in the room would easily get the distinct impression of eating their meal amidst of the eighteenth century.

Upon arriving to his room, Kyran gave Josh a healthy tip for the trouble. He thought the kid was going to fall back and faint at the sight of the ten-dollar bill. Any second and Kyran was sure the kid was going to fall on his knees and kiss his feet. It took several minutes to convince the kid he was relieved of his duties and it wasn't necessary for him to turn back the bed, or get him ice, or do anything else for that matter. Nonetheless, Kyran was assured a friend in Josh should the need arise.

Once he shut the door behind the grinning teen, he sat down on the four-poster bed and looked the room over. It was done up in the same old-fashioned mode as the rest of the inn. He got up and went over to the bureau mirror to have a look at himself.

"Not very appealing," he said aloud. "If your agent got a

look at you now, he'd want to buy out quick."

He slipped a cigarette out of the pack he kept in his pocket, lit a match, shook it out and tossed it into the complimentary ashtray he found sitting on top of the bureau. He dropped the pack down beside the ashtray.

I've gotta quit these things, he thought. *Not so much in style anymore anyway. Never mind how they appear to help the masculine image. It won't do me any good if I'm not around to enjoy it.*

He took a couple of drags, breathing in deeply, and snuffed the cigarette out. The couple of puffs were enough to soothe the need which had erupted due to the stress of the situation.

"Okay, buddy," he said as he inspected himself in the mirror. "Prince Charming you're not, but it'll have to do. You can fix yourself up fine when you've got a little more time."

He checked his pocket for his keys and turned to leave. After a moment's hesitation, he grabbed the pack of cigarettes and stuck them back in his pocket. He was going to the police station, and he knew he wouldn't last without them. Regardless of how restrained he wanted himself to be, nervousness and anxiousness were in control of his attitude, and he needed the cigarettes to help him unwind.

Chapter Six

Hyram Beckham was a conscientious police chief who took his duties to heart. His manner was easy going but serious enough when it was important.

He was broad shouldered and heavily built with a military-type crew cut. At first glance, those who met him thought him to be a mean tempered individual, but soon found him to be friendly, polite and overly helpful, leading them into falsely thinking him to be naïve, a sucker. They'd attempt to whittle their way out of tickets or misdemeanors by lying through their teeth. Chief Beckham played their game, whittling tricks of his own magic silently and slyly, eventually taking them by surprise with how smart and sharp he really was, a real tough cookie no one could take for a ride. Chief Beckham surprised the hell out of hardcore criminals in his time who at first thought they were on easy street, but soon found out the true nature of things once the chief got their face under a bright light for questioning. He was good at his job, and he prided himself for it.

The day was fairly crimeless. Nothing big had arisen, and Hyram was glad for it. He liked it when things were boring, because it meant less for him to get stressed out about.

Middlebury was a pretty good place to work. He applied for the position there when he turned sixty, nearing retirement. Previously stationed at a precinct in Killington, Vermont where trouble went with a capital 'T', he wanted to ensure he reached retirement age.

Killington drew all kinds of people from all over the United States in swarms. Anybody who was anybody at skiing eventually made their way to Killington, which had some of the best ski slopes in the world, and sponsored contest and competitions for money. Unfortunately, that meant drawing money hungry people, as well, and they brought trouble right in with them.

After spending his entire career in Killington and surviving many a rough time, Hyram felt his luck was quickly running out. He didn't want to be another statistic, ending up on a list of names with other brave officers who died in the line of fire just short of retirement. When he put in for Middlebury, he made certain he did his homework right.

Middlebury's population wasn't very large, and the only time real trouble arose was when out-of-towners came for the summer season. Ninety percent of the time, they were the culprits responsible for the messy stuff that occurred around town. Ordinary town folk merely wrestled in family bustles, and the college students wrestled in barroom brawls.

Today, like most days, there wasn't much to speak of. Nosirree. Except for the fact it was steadily raining outside, as it had been for the last couple of days, making driving difficult due to slippery roads. The sun made only a brief appearance early that morning, and then returned behind the clouds to hide. Winter winds, having arrived prematurely, helped to make driving conditions worse, and Hyram had several car collisions to fend with throughout the day thus far.

Of course, one of every two cars involved in an accident belonged to an out-of-towner who inevitably was responsible for the collision in the first place. The all-year-round people knew how to drive when this kind of weather hit the Middlebury area, but out-of-towners either had no idea what it was like, or simply didn't give a hoot. It was a shame, too, the Middlebury folk having to suffer for their ignorance.

Hyram was sitting at his desk with his feet propped and crossed over the desk top surface, reading over a file pertaining to a local couple. The wife was requesting a restraining order against her husband who was physically abusing her for several months.

He was making marginal notations when a voice cut across him, scattering his thoughts.

"Excuse me."

He looked up to see the face of the famous Kyran Cornell looking down at him. He was utterly taken by surprise. It just so happened the previous Saturday night, Hyram and his wife Thelma went to see the opening of his new film. He motioned for Kyran to sit down.

The sight of Kyran's boyish grin made him look honest and forthcoming, but after listening to the odd tale he told, Hyram wondered whether he could believe the man or not. He'd always pictured the young man to be level-headed in real life, but his story seemed to be missing a lot of important details.

"Let me see if I unnerstand ya correctly, Mr. Cornell," Hyram began, measuring Kyran with an uneasy look. "This here lady you claim to be missin' is a gal you met at a party. You don't know her name, only what she looks like. You wanted to ask her out on a date. So, you called the friend who innerduced ya to her, and he said he heard she up and went missin' for a coupla days and last he unnerstood was she mentioned somethin' 'bout headin' to Middlebury, Vermont?" His voice drawled on nonchalantly in a dry, Vermont twang. Hyram yawned and rubbed his neck with weariness.

"Yes Sir," Kyran responded with a cough. He appeared to be self-conscious. He was constantly running his hand through his hair and adjusting his jacket. "I know it sounds totally ridiculous, but I was extremely attracted to her. We got along quite well." Kyran scratched the back of his head and went for his pack of cigarettes. "Is it okay to smoke?" he asked.

Chief Beckham nodded, then continued. "And you mean to say this here *friend* didn't innerduce you to her by name? And you traveled all this way from New York jest to find 'er?" He pretended to be only half-listening.

"Yes, Sir," Kyran answered firmly, sounding impatient and moistening his lips with his tongue. "I mean, he did say her name, but I didn't hear it and was too embarrassed to ask again."

"What makes you think she might be in any kind of danger anyways?" Chief Beckham inquired, intensely chewing on a hangnail on his index finger wondering the whole time if Kyran even realized how dumb the statement sounded. Judging by the look on his face, Chief Beckham thought he did!

Kyran already lit a cigarette and was flicking the ashes into the palm of his hand. Chief Beckham handed him a Styrofoam coffee cup with a bit of liquid still in it. Kyran took it from his outstretched hand.

Kyran was clearly nervous. "I know it sounds peculiar to you, chief, but I really liked her. It's hard to find a good woman nowadays, you know? Call it a storybook fairytale if you want, but...." He paused to think his response through. "You see, Sir, I'm a bit of what you call *psychic*." Kyran awkwardly took his eyes away from the chief's.

"It's kind of like when someone is about to board a plane, but at the very last-minute changes their mind, 'cause they have a funny feeling something bad is going to happen." He said this almost teary-eyed. "I can't seem to shake the feeling she might be in danger, and I'd like to find her and put my mind to rest. Plus, I'm pretty confident I could have a future with this young lady if given the chance." He finished.

"*Psychic*, you say?" Hyram prompted. He raised his eyebrows high, rubbing his chin, pondering the situation. He didn't necessarily believe the psychic part of it, though he was tempted to use one or two in cases over the years, but being a romantic-at-heart, he felt sorry for the guy. Even if it was a desperate tall tale in order to find the woman, it couldn't hurt if Hyram helped him out some. After all, Kyran Cornell was a well-known figure, and it'd be difficult for him to *disappear* in Middlebury. The town was only six square miles.

He decided he'd see what he could do, but he'd keep a tight rein on the situation, *and* on Mr. Cornell.

"Alright, Mr. Cornell," he finally answered. "Let me go recheck today's bulletins and see if I can't help you out."

"Thank you," Kyran said, talking through a cloud of hazy smoke, excitement obvious in his voice. "I really do appreciate it."

Hyram held up his hand to shush him. "Don't thank me yet. This don't mean you're off the hook entirely. You make certain to keep close by in case I need to find ya. Ya hear?"

"Of course," Kyran nodded eagerly.

"And, uh," Hyram added. "If'n it all works out in the end, then you send me a formal thank you."

"Uh, yes, Sir," Kyran said, clearing his throat and blushing.

Chief Beckham walked swiftly out of his office and over to the board where the latest bulletins were posted and started to scan them over.

Usually before his shift began, he'd read through the latest bulletins to get a grip on what to look for in the days ahead, always keeping on top of things, going back to the board two and three times a day to see about new additions, and doing regular follow-ups on them, as well. He looked them over at 5:30 that morning. This was his second visit there.

It was several minutes before he went back to where Kyran waited, puzzling over one of the latest bulletins in his hand. He was perplexed. He sat down in his desk chair.

"Well, looky here," he said, puckering his face. "Mmm-mmm."

Kyran listened patiently when Hyram finally looked up and said, "Mr. Cornell, I think you might have something here."

Kyran sat up straight, leaning toward Officer Beckham's desk.

Any further and he'd have fallen over.

"Seems a lady fittin' the description you gave me was admitted to Middlebury Hospital jest his mornin' around eight. Fits yer description purdy damn well, iff'n I say so myself."

His eyes met Kyran's with a challenging stare.

"Middlebury Hospital?" Kyran asked, already on his feet.

"Yes," said Chief Beckham. Kyran was halfway out the door. The Chief abruptly called out to him. "Mr. Cornell!"

Kyran stopped dead in his tracks and hesitantly turned around.

"Middlebury Hospital is on the other side of town."

Kyran nodded, taking a few steps out the door, but Chief Beckham persisted; authority clear in his voice, "And, Mr. Cornell...."

Kyran stopped again without turning around this time.

"Don't you go forgettin' what I said about keepin' close by."

"I won't," Kyran said. "And, thank you."

After watching Kyran leave, Hyram picked up the phone to call Middlebury Hospital, but changed his mind and hung up.

I'll jest wait and see what comes up in the next few days, he thought to himself with a sigh and shake of his head. *I ain't got nuthin' to worry about with this lovestruck sucker anyways.*

***

It took Kyran less than seven minutes to reach the other side of town. Finally, at Middlebury Hospital, he immediately headed for the emergency ward. As he walked through its double doors, he found twenty people seated in chairs scattered throughout its smelly, disinfected waiting area.

On his way to the admittance desk, he passed a teenage boy who was holding several bloodied towels up to his left ear. Kyran's stomach churned. It wasn't strong enough to withstand the sight of so much blood. *What a hero!*

The admittance desk was momentarily unmanned, and Kyran stood patiently waiting.

He watched as a young girl, probably a babysitter, painstakingly try to quiet a screaming, red-faced infant.

Opposite her, an elderly woman lay with her head in the lap of an elderly man who repeatedly caressed her cheek saying, "Everything will be alright, Miriam. It's going to be just fine."

The elderly woman continued to moan in response.

The telephone behind the counter rang, startling Kyran alert, and a full-figured nurse ran in to pick it up.

From behind a nearby closed door, a woman clearly in labor was yelling, "Don't fucking touch me, you bastard! Don't fucking touch me ever again! You did this to me! You bastard! You *b-a-s-t-a-r-d*!"

Her husband could be heard trying to soothe her with calming responses.

"Just a little more to go, honey. Not much longer."

Embarrassed, Kyran pretended not to be listening. Moments later, a slap and a scream arose in the air as the newborn was brought into the world, followed by a murmuring of words.

"It's a boy! Congratulations."

"He's beautiful."

"Oh, honey, I love you!"

Kyran raised his eyebrows and smiled at the old man. A beautiful moment until the old man opened his mouth and exclaimed, "Yup. Another hoodlum born to this stinkpot of a country."

Kyran abruptly looked away from him, hoping to capture the attention of the full-figured nurse, who had hung up the phone and was now involved in a deep conversation with an orderly over the soap opera, *The Young and the Restless*.

Becoming increasingly impatient, Kyran released a sigh of frustration. He loudly cleared his throat in another attempt to get her to look his way. He desperately wanted to inquire about the woman admitted there earlier. Kyran's gut feeling was that she was The Woman of his Dream. He devised a story but wasn't sure how well it would work.

As luck would have it, the nurse made it easy for him. When she finally turned away from the orderly, she immediately recognized his face and was aghast with surprise, her previous conversation immediately forgotten.

She began raving about how wonderful an actor she thought he was, and how she'd seen all his movies. Normally, Kyran hated the attention that went with being a celebrity, but this time he was grateful for it. It meant not having to go into the scenario he prepared. All he needed to do was ask if any Jane Does had been admitted, and she took it upon herself to inform him a woman patient whose identity was unknown was admitted earlier that morning. It clearly didn't dawn on her the woman could very well be his dying wife, and here she was raving about how wonderful he was. She had the audacity to ask Kyran for his autograph, but Kyran obliged, using it as a ploy to get in to see Jane Doe. The nurse led the way without mishap, totally engrossed in being in the presence of a star. She even failed to ask for any pertinent information.

She yip-yapped the entire way as she walked beside Kyran to the woman's room. He simply smiled, pretending to pay strict attention to her conversation when, really, he tuned her out altogether. He was too preoccupied with the probability of actually coming in contact with The Woman of his Dream.

Kyran practically shat his pants as they approached the room, getting nearer and nearer.

Can this truly be happening? He wasn't one hundred percent sure and wouldn't believe it either until he saw her face. There was still the chance it might not be The Woman, and all of this could've been a wild goose chase on the part of a man going crazy. But he remained optimistic.

"This is her room, Mr. Cornell," the nurse said. "If I can be of any further assistance, please don't hesitate to ask me. My name is Madge."

"Thanks, Madge," Kyran responded. "I'll be sure to do that."

He waited for her to walk off, watching as she turned around to steal one last look at him. From this day on, he was assured a Number One Fan. Before the day was through, he knew every person she came in contact with would know what a kindly individual the movie star, Kyran Cornell, was.

She left him at Room 46. Kyran stood in front of the closed door, his nose nearly touching its white surface. He felt the sweat building on his brow and took a few deep breaths to help regain his composure. In his mind, he clearly heard her whisper-cry his name. The more he considered it, the more certain he became that it must be The Woman.

Please God, let It be her.

He bit the side of his lip as his hand grasped the doorknob and turned it. Waiting several seconds to build up the nerve and necessary energy, he pushed the door inward.

And, there she was.

The Woman.

Bruised and broken.

But it was her.

It blew his mind. The realization that none of it had been his overblown imagination astounded him. His mental well-being was no longer in question.

Kyran summoned up further courage and slowly walked over to her bedside. Though she was extensively bandaged, black and blue, and in total disarray, it was without a doubt her.

But who was she? Would he ever find out?

At least he could be happy for having found her at all. He was one step ahead. From here on in, everything else could wait. One day at a time. That was the way to do it.

He pulled up a chair and sat down next to her. She was the only patient in the room. Probably because the circumstances of her dilemma warranted it, or simply because the hospital had the room.

He looked at her, and although he didn't know her name, he felt he'd known her his entire life. The sight of her acutely affected him.

The Woman of The Dream.

Although no memories were shared between them except those created in The Dream, he felt connected to her, bonded to her.

The incessant need to cry overwhelmed him, but he held it in check. He wasn't sure if he wanted to cry because of her condition or because he finally found her and his sanity along with it.

Kyran was sitting there for quite some time when the door to her room opened and a doctor walked in.

"Mr. Cornell, I presume?" he asked, stopping directly in front of Kyran. "My name is Dr. Winthrop. Nurse Nelson informed me you were here."

He was a tall man of about six-foot-three and one hundred and ninety pounds, slim and trim, with a head of flaxen, curly hair, and appeared to be in his late thirties. He had a demure air of authority about him representative of the M.D. after his name.

Kyran stood up to shake the doctor's hand.

"How is she, doctor?"

"Well, I must admit, she's a very lucky lady," he said. "She's been through an awful lot, and it's not entirely over yet either." Dr. Winthrop looked Kyran over speculatively. "I'm curious to know your connection to this woman. I'm concerned about notifying any family members she has."

"I'm afraid I can't help you there, doctor," Kyran began, coughing to clear his throat. He told him the same story he told Chief Beckham earlier. "It's really sheer luck she's the same woman I came looking for."

Dr. Winthrop's eyes studied Kyran cautiously. "I'm going to be perfectly honest with you, Mr. Cornell," he said. "I pride myself in being a good judge of people, and I'm not in the habit of compromising my position for the *sheer luck* of it. If not for the fact she spoke your name out loud before lapsing into a coma, I wouldn't help you in the least. Celebrity or not."

He stood up straight, holding his head high as if throwing his weight around; his mouth turning down the corners.

"She called out my name?" Kyran asked, stunned.

86

"Yes, she did," he answered. "And, I'm still at odds about the story you've told me, but she didn't *scream* your name, she *spoke* it. That to me is a positive sign, and it puts me on your side for the time being, unless it becomes apparent you played a role in putting her in her present the condition."

"You can't think I had anything to do with—" Kyran was flabbergasted by the implication. "What are you talking ab--?"

"But," Dr. Winthrop abruptly interjected, "I do take into consideration you traveled far to find her—whatever your reasons—and you seem honestly concerned about her. And, you haven't taken any pains to conceal your identity in any way. Not that I think you could even if you tried." He smirked.

"My position implores me to advise you to be wary, Mr. Cornell. I'm also on the side of the police in finding out her identity and capturing her assailant. Normal injuries would indicate it was an accident, but this wasn't merely an accident. Something led up to it, and she sustained a stab wound in the interim. This clearly is foul play. If I have any suspicions you are involved in any way whatsoever, rest assured I will do everything in my power to see you pay for it. I'm in the business of *saving* lives, Mr. Cornell, and I intend to do just that!" He looked Kyran squarely in the face.

"I can assure you, doctor," Kyran began coldly, "that I had nothing whatsoever to do with harming her, and I have only her best interests at heart."

His face turned red with a slight tinge of anger which instantly dissipated.

He's a doctor who is concerned about his patient, Kyran reasoned. *Of course, he's going to ask questions and make logical assumptions. It's his job.*

"I can verify my whereabouts, if necessary, and I've already been in touch with Chief Beckham at the Middlebury Police. However farfetched you may think my story is, I care about the welfare of this woman, and I *will* be as cooperative as possible."

"Very well. As long as we understand one another," the doctor responded firmly. "You appear to genuinely care for her, and I'll give you every consideration. Since you seem to be the only person who knows her to any extent, I will try to be as cooperative with you, as well."

"Thank you," Kyran said, breathing a sigh of relief. "I appreciate your concern and certainly understand the full extent of it."

He was glad the preliminary hearing was over, and he had passed.

"As I mentioned, she's been through a tremendous ordeal, and because of it, has developed an infection and fever," Dr. Winthrop explained, shaking his head from side to side. "Anybody having to deal with the extreme conditions of the weather—the rain and cold—along with the degree of her injuries, and still come out alive…"

He was clearly astounded by her incredible will to live.

"She most definitely should be considered lucky. Of course, no one can tell how long she was out in the cold. The gentleman who found her in the back of his truck said it could've been as long as ten hours."

"Ten hours?" Kyran repeated dumbfounded. "If I only got here sooner."

He felt himself sinking deeper and deeper into a feeling of helplessness.

The doctor continued. "She lapsed into a coma due to a massive concussion and loss of blood. Aside from a number of cuts and abrasions, she was stabbed once in the lower abdomen and has a foot injury, all of which are healing properly. I'm not certain if she sustained any brain injury and won't know until she comes out of the coma, if she ever does. So, you see, Mr. Cornell, the worst isn't over yet. I remain quite skeptical."

"Thank you for taking me into your confidence and trust, doctor," Kyran said. "I'm not going anywhere. I intend to stay around. If you need me at all, I'll make sure you know where to find me."

Kyran half expected the doctor to offer his hand for a shake, but it didn't happen.

"Very good," Dr. Winthrop said. "I'll keep you advised on her progress."

He turned and left the room, leaving Kyran to sit beside The Woman from The Dream.

To wonder.

And hope.

***

Ripping open the paper wrapper of one of the Mars Bars left over from the remaining bag of food he found in the old man's Chevy, Emilio took small bites, eating it slowly, savoring its smooth flavor. Having already consumed the hero and slaw, he was eating the candy bar for enjoyment and not hunger. He concentrated his attention on finding another car in order to make a switch.

The rain subsided, but it wouldn't be long before it began again.

Although the air was brisk and nippy, Emilio opened the car window to let it in. He was feeling warm, and the breeze was contenting to the touch.

As he drove on Route 739 in Pennsylvania, he slowed down to

survey the parking lot of a saloon called *The Red Eagle*. A Buick Regal pulled out as he pulled in. It was the only moving car in sight. There were eight cars parked in the front open area of the lot and four on a concealed, unlit portion off to the side.

A woman came out from the saloon's entrance. She was alone and clearly drunk by the way she staggered in her six-inch high heels, making her way to the concealed side lot. A hint of a red dress peeked through the bottom of her leather jacket.

Emilio's luck was at work again. Shudders of excitement permeated his loins.

The woman fumbled around in a red shoulder bag she was carrying. Its shade matched perfectly with her shoes. Even this appeared to be a difficult task for her. She squinted her eyes and shoved the bag under her nose in a lame attempt to located something, probably her keys. The bag slipped from her grasp, and several pieces of its contents fell to the ground. She made a feeble attempt to retrieve them, losing her red shoe in the process, and leaving a package of tissues behind. She managed to slip her shoe back on and, faltering momentarily, return to a wobbly stand.

Emilio got out of the Chevy with his hand in his pocket wrapped firmly around his blade, ready to use it. He looked about to make sure no one else was watching him.

The woman stopped beside a blue Toronado. She was fervently focusing the key in the direction of the lock without any success.

Emilio swiftly moved in.

Concentrating on hitting her mark, the woman barely had time to turn her head before Emilio grabbed her by her hair and stuck the knife into the side of her neck, breaking her windpipe, making her choke on her own blood. Within seconds it was over.

Looking around to make certain he was still unobserved he lifted the woman off the ground. Her red bag dangled from her shoulder but didn't fall. He picked the keys up off the ground where she'd dropped them in the brief struggle, unlocked the trunk, and dropped her body in it. He grabbed a blanket from inside the back of the trunk and stuffed it under the open wound in an attempt to plug up the flow of blood.

Her eyes were closed. Except for the gigantic hole in her neck gushing blood, she appeared to be sleeping peacefully, her head resting casually on its side on the blanket as if in the throngs of an evening nap.

Later he would dispose of the body, as he'd done with all the others. He needed to ensure no link could be made between any of them. Now, he needed to continue moving, changing cars every so often, something he became accustomed to. This was his life, and he knew it well.

He hurriedly slammed the trunk lid and jumped into the driver's side of the car.

He was grateful for his good fortune. Normally, without keys, he'd have to hammer at the ignition switch, fighting with it for several l-o-n-g moments, until finally breaking the key plate loose from the steering column, all the while keeping an eye open for passersby. Then, pull out the ignition wires, cross the two bare ends, and pump gently on the accelerator until the engine started. It took time to pull off, and required extreme patience, something which he was heavily lacking in of late. And, it wasn't an easy thing to do when under duress of possibly being discovered.

I am so damned lucky, he thought.

Another sign of the good fate dealt to him, and him alone. Destiny was such a wonderful thing. Emilio was positive of his special role in life. This incident, added to the long list of others, was proof of the fact. He was definitely on his way to culminating his destiny, as long as he's satisfied the never-ending Need within him.

His Need. Demands. Fulfillment.

Search. Catch. Kill.

His ultimate purpose in life.

Until.

Until the time when he wouldn't have to take what he needed, but it would be given to him freely. He'd sit on his throne, high above a pedestal, as victims stood before him offering themselves willingly. He'd accept it with pleasure, basking in their blood as it flowed from their loins in waves of crimson red.

While driving, he reminisced about the very first day he understood what his purpose in life was.

It had been a cold, wintry day in the middle of Emilio's twenty-first year on earth. He was in the snow-covered mountains of Colorado when he found himself in the throes of one of his urges for bloody slaughter and went out in search of his prey to unleash it.

He abducted two sisters, about nine and twelve years old from their sleigh riding spree and took them to a secluded part of the woods. He recalled it hadn't been difficult at all. He merely promised the oldest girl he wouldn't hurt them if they obeyed. Then, he was amazed at how easy it all was. The oldest listened and didn't fight back, because she saw how frightened her young sister was. She allowed herself to be tied up, instructing her sister to do the same. She trusted Emilio wouldn't harm them if they complied. She trusted the wrong person.

Emilio was appalled by the elder's strong need to protect her baby sister, contempt pinching his nerves. He vowed to make her pay for it.

After tying both girls up, he made good on his intention and forced the older girl into watching as he killed her younger sister, slowly draining the life from her. He was thrilled by the terrified look on her face as he submitted her to viewing his ejaculating over her bleeding corpse.

Then, as he slit the older girl's throat, a voice from within her staring, blank eyes encouraged him to drink of her blood. He did, finding in it a newfound hope and understanding.

The voice informed him then that one day he would be rewarded for his efforts; he was The Chosen One. It was his fate.

It told him the girl should've understood why she was there. She had been given to his as a gift. People were still blind to the faith, but the time would come when they'd all know their proper place and recognize the immensity of his stature. Now, they were too blind to see their own arrogance.

As if to ensure the consummation was irrevocable, Emilio left behind is mark and pissed atop both bodies before leaving them to freeze in the wintry night.

It was a wondrous day of reckoning for him, the happiest day of his life to have observed such an important revelation.

It was on that day he realized he was *somebody* after always believing he was a worthless *nobody*. But, how could he not have believed such a thing with everyone always telling him so?

As a child, his mother and father beat him continuously, yelling he should never have been born, the high content of alcohol within their system revealing the true nature of their feelings.

Time and time again, overhearing his teachers tell his parents he would never amount to anything. Even though he couldn't hear their conversations directly, he knew. Somehow, he knew what they were really saying all along.

And the policemen who confined and captured him revealing their true feelings with the look in their eyes and the way in which they treated him.

Even the preacher he went to for help when he was eleven years old turned him away. He needed help desperately. When he honestly believed he finally was getting the help he sought, the man asked for sex. Emilio refused, and the holy one yelled at him, screaming he was nothing but a low-life scum, not worthy of his attention.

After joining up with a clan of others like himself, he grew bolder, eventually returning confidently to the parish of St. Frances de Chantal and showing Fr. Graham who the real scum was. He remembered so clearly how the man of cloth begged for his life, but instead Emilio cut off the man's penis, stuck it in his mouth, and left him to bleed to death. Even then, Emilio somehow sensed he was special.

From the day the voice entered his life, it became his constant companion, and Emilio christened it *Crater.*

Crater was all-knowing and wise in many respects, teaching him well, and Emilio carried out its gruesome requests with aplomb, grace and joy, taking as much, if not more, gratification from them as Crater did. This was the antidote to the growing Need within his soul.

Behind the wheel of the Toronado, Emilio remembered and smiled.

Things were looking better and better. His day was close at hand. He could feel it; sense glory and prestige gaining closer. It was coming.

It was coming.

Coming.

Even though the woman's cadaver lay bleeding in the Toronado's trunk, Emilio accelerated without worry. Nothing could touch him now.

Nothing. It was his fate.

***

Forty-eight hours. She's been gone for forty-eight hours.

Adam couldn't believe it. Could she have gotten the gumption to leave him after all? He didn't believe she had it in her.

He poured himself another cup of coffee and went back into the living room to sit down and contemplate the situation.

Victoria hadn't been home when he arrived from his regular rendezvous with Lina, but he thought nothing of it. Several hours passed and she still hadn't shown. He began to assume she left him.

But she doesn't have the guts, Adam thought. *Does she?*

He checked the mantelpiece for a *Dear John* letter but found none. Nor had she taken any of her belongings.

Would she be that stupid?

Adam didn't think so.

Now, forty-eight hours later, he wasn't sure what to think. He leaned back in his comfortable, upholstered chair, sinking into its soft cushions, and laid his head back. Relaxing, he sipped black, steaming coffee from his mug. He already finished four full pots of coffee, something he enjoyed doing while in a thinking mode. During the younger years of his career, he got a fondness for it. Over the years, he graduated from three to four cups a day, to three to four pots instead. Tonight, was an exception to the rule. He was overly tense.

He tried to relax and closed his eyes. Kenny G's instrumental, *Songbird*, filled the air around him bringing with it a distinct memory. It was the song he chose as the background music for his and Victoria's wedding video. At the time, he chose it specifically because it was the only appropriate selection. There weren't any words to it. Words painted pictures of emotions, especially tender and poignant ones. He hadn't wanted that. He hadn't wanted that at all.

At least when Victoria forced him to view the video for whatever inane reason, Adam focused his eyes above the screen and simply listened to the instruments, enrapturing himself with the rhythmic sound of the music, creating a mental picture of his own derision.

Time was moving quickly. Adam supposed he should make a call to the local police. He knew he'd have to inform them of the possibility she had deserted him. After all, they hadn't been living in marital bliss. He merely tolerated Victoria for argument's sake. Victoria might've considered it normal behavior, but Adam though differently. He suspected she might know about his affairs, but she never mentioned it to him.

She was too weak to be bold. Nonetheless, he'd have to make the call all the same. Perhaps she'd be found dead somewhere, not that it really mattered. It that were to happen, all his problems would be instantly solved. Since marrying her three years before, he was now sorry he chose her. She was too sensitive for her own good. She wanted things like love and romance, something which he gave freely in the beginning in order to win her over, something which he wouldn't be stupid enough to do again. He had no interest in either one. He only craved personal gratification. He was rich. Therefore, in order to find an appropriate replacement, it wasn't necessary to do any of that.

Victoria was easily replaceable. There were more of her where she came from. Most women were cut from the same mold. Like his father always told him, "Five more like her, then you've got six."

He'd pick another. Only the one he chose would be more compliant to his needs, one willing to do what he wanted her to do for money's sake. Adam wasn't the least bit concerned.

He propped his elbow on the arm of his chair, nervously playing with his chin, another habit he had developed for when he was involved in serious thought. He unconsciously crossed and uncrossed his legs, careful to avoid wrinkling his suit pants. He was always impeccably dressed and well-groomed, something he invariably carried out in his home, as well.

In an average household, it usually was the woman who took a lengthy amount of time getting ready, but in the Sheldon household, it was Adam. He was slow in the process of dressing, because he needed to make certain his clothing fit just right and was properly pressed. Aside from the normal hygiene routine, he took unusually long showers in the morning and spent a good hour grooming his hair, moustache, and beard. An extra ten minutes or so was applied to plucking newly sprouted nose hairs.

Preparation for him was a ritual he adhered to. With a reputation to uphold, and a distinct impression to present to the public, it was the number one priority on his list. Which was why he was so intimately thinking about Victoria's disappearance. He had to prepare for how he would handle the situation.

He hesitantly leaned across the end-table to life the receiver from the handset, lazily resting his elbow atop the grainy wood surface. He dialed nine-one-one.

Better do it right, he thought.

It was necessary to file a missing person's report. Otherwise, he'd appear suspicious in case foul play was involved. He'd have to be careful not to do anything rash, chance jeopardizing his reputation and risk becoming the target of public scorn. With his high position, he couldn't afford to do that. Not showing concern was undignified and didn't look good. But, if foul play was involved, he couldn't have thought of a better way of doing it himself. He was excited by the prospect of hunting down a new wife, but he didn't want to get overly anxious just in case she was still alive.

He waited impatiently as the connection was made. Patting the open palm of his left hand onto his left thigh, he listened, frustrated, as the phone continued to ring at the other end. The operator finally picked up the line after eight rings. Typical. Adam was surprised he got a live person and not a machine telling him all lines were busy and to try back later.

"Yes," he said. "My name is Adam Sheldon, and I would like to report my wife as missing."

Chapter Seven

"Optimism is one of the secrets to a happy life."
--Kyran Cornell

Kyran was aware the doctors and their staff offered a daily update on The Woman's condition out of respect for his amazing perseverance. She was in the same state for almost a week with little or no improvement and no sign of coming out of the coma.

Kyran worked tediously, reading to her from magazines and books, talking about inane things, telling her about his life, inner sensitivity guiding him. He hoped somehow deep within the recesses of the coma world she might hear him, even if in tiny whispers, and want to come out to be with him.

As he sat in the same metal chair he'd been sitting in day after day since her admission, he glanced around the room.

The television set sat temporarily unused high atop a swivel shelf oddly attached to a hanging bar off the ceiling.

A bulletin board normally used for cards from well-wishers hung empty on the wall; a sad reminder of The Woman's dilemma, almost proclaiming her non-existent, though Kyran knew better.

A container of ice water, brought in specifically for his use, lay untouched on a serving table against the wall, droplets of water running down its side. On the nightstand sat the latest book he'd been reading from to The Woman. It was *Little House on the Prairie* by Laura Ingalls Wilder. Kyran didn't know why he selected it. He supposed it was in hopes of jarring her awake with some wonderful childhood memory similar to the main character in the book. He wasn't sure if it would work, but anything was worth a try. Next week he might resort to a Dean Koontz novel and frighten her from her coma-sleep.

Day in and day out, when this whole bizarre thing started, he thought he was losing control of his life. The Dream made it appear so, but then things took a dramatic turn. The Woman gave his life a distinct purpose. He'd help her overcome this. He wouldn't fail. He'd *make*, her, *Goddamnit!* He had to. No matter how long it took.

Kyran ran his hand through his hair and twisted his neck to get the annoying cricks out. Although he went back to the inn to sleep most nights, he fell asleep just as often in the metal chair beside her bed. Because of it, his neck and lower back were sore. He leaned back and sighed.

"Who are you," he asked, rubbing his weary eyes, looking for a sign of movement from her still form.

Still, no one knew her name. She was only known to him and the rest of the hospital staff as *Jane Doe*. Kyran hired private detectives to find out her real identity, and they were combing every possibility. They worked diligently, searching for an identity to match her description.

Having accessed the police department's data banks, Police Chief Beckham informed Kyran of thirty women listed among the missing persons list from the beginning of the year, but none of them fit the description of Jane Doe. He was kind enough to keep Kyran abreast of any fresh developments in the search, but to date, there weren't any. It seemed all efforts were futile and led only to a dead-end pass.

The daily update on the investigation's status left Kyran frustrated and depressed. Now, as he watched her silent form wrapped in bandages, with tubes protruding from her body, he wasn't sure if they would ever know who she was, and she might never wake up from her unnatural sleep to tell them.

"Who are you?" Kyran asked aloud.

Aside from being tired, Kyran was restless and weak. He'd been wearing the same shirt now for three days with no spirit to change it. It looked as if it was once blue, but was now faded to a bland, dark gray having been through a dozen or so washings. Wet circles of perspiration soaked through his underarms, appearing atop others that dried and left their mark days before—out of the ordinary from his normally well-kept appearance and hygiene. His sleeves were rolled up to his elbows. He felt dirty and in need of a shower, even though he took one that morning.

The moonlight through the hospital room window cast dancing shadows across The Woman's immobile form on the bed. Kyran watched the steady rise and fall of her chest.

At least she's breathing on her own, he thought.

Optimism. Very important. It's one of the secrets to leading a happy life. As long as one is optimistic, worry cannot penetrate the mind and interfere with the natural swing of things. The need to look forward to better things is strong.

Kyran worked diligently to convince himself.

Except Kyran was sadly beginning to doubt his own motto.

He walked over to the window, half unconsciously leaning against the frame, and looked out at the night's sky. Outside, the town was bathed in white and yellow lights of cars in motion and the glow coming from inside peoples' homes. The weather hadn't changed. The rain continued, only stopping for a few hours at a time. According to the weather report, the rainy weather would continue through mid-week. It was almost as if The Woman was controlling a weather dial which she set to whatever preference she had, and because of her dire condition, she chose a black cloud hovering above her, releasing rain to mimic the tears of anguish she felt inside.

As if in confirmation of Kyran's theory, the rain made its presence known by dropping tiny specs of water against the hospital window.

Kyran's face was so close to the windowpane that his nose touched its cold, wet surface and his breath left a trailing mark of fog.

He thought about The Woman. Jane Doe.

It must be peaceful living in a world devoid of people and machinery: the congestion and sounds of daily living.

That's probably why she doesn't want to wake up. With a nurse or orderly coming in each day to take care of the necessities for her, she doesn't have a care in the world.

Then why would she reach out to me for help? There must be a specific reason for that, right?

He let the hospital curtain drop back into place. He spoke to her with his mind.

Why don't you come to me again?

He reflected upon the night she paid him a visit. She appeared ghost-like; floating in the darkness. The deep-seated dread he felt then suddenly rushed back to him in a hail of burning bullets.

Was it an out-of-body experience? Were you somehow responsible for the dreams I've been having all along?

He desperately wanted to know. He needed to know, but the only way to find out would be to have her awaken to tell him. Since that time, she never visited again, and The Dream ceased as though it never existed. Maybe she no longer was able to summon up the power to transmit The Dream to him, or maybe she no longer wanted to.

Kyran refused to believe the latter.

He picked up the book to read from it. He needed to focus his mind on something other than The Woman. Reading the story would help him to do that. He opened to the page he ended on and began to read aloud. "Laura felt a soft warmth on her face and opened her eyes into morning sunshine. Mary was talking to ma."

He read on for about an hour until he became too tired to continue. Then, he folded the book into his lap and leaned over to pick up the television remote, flicking it on to a *Star Trek* repeat. He watched it until he fell asleep once again on the uncomfortable, metal chair beside her bed.

***

Coming to a three-way intersection with a Dunkin Donuts on the right, Emilio decided to pull in and take a break.

TIME TO EAT THE DONUTS, Crater intoned from within. *WHO THE FUCK CARES WHO BAKED 'EM? HARDY-HAR-HAR.*

Emilio heard his stomach growling in exclamation to Crater's remark. He ordered a box of Munchkins and two dozen mixed donuts, some of which he'd save for his ride ahead. He paid with the cash he'd taken from the dead woman's red shoulder bag.

"Looks like somebody's having company," said the smiling blonde-haired register girl. She reminded Emilio of a Barbie Doll.

"Oh, really, who?" Emilio responded curtly, feigning stupidity and walked off.

He stayed briefly, selecting a table by the window, pondering over his successes to date. As he stuffed a powdered blueberry-filled donut into his mouth, he delighted in the manner which he pulled off every murder. He easily could've compared himself to such greats as The Black Dahlia Murderer or Jeffrey Dahmer. He was optimistic by the progress he was making, but knew he was running out of time and needed to be quick about making the appropriate preparations.

Now, slowly munching on a plain cruller, he realized he was tired and needed to get some rest. He went too long without sleeping, all due to Crater's constant insistence to fulfill The Need.

The attack on the woman in Vernon, the old man in Lafayette, and the red lady in Pennsylvania all took their toll on him, draining him of every ounce of energy and depleting any reserve tank resources he had left.

In the beginning, there was several months between killings. Over the years the time separating killings became less and less. Within the last six months, there had been no separation at all. Whenever The Need struck him, he proceeded to fulfill it. During the last three weeks, The Need was incessant, barely leaving Emilio time to breathe. He hoped the sugar level in the donuts was enough to force rejuvenation.

Although The Need was thoroughly satisfied, it left him weak, in desperate need of refueling his body if he was to continue on. The demands of The Need continually progressed with each day; Crater's voice becoming louder and louder, more forceful.

NEED. DEMANDS. FULFILLMENT.

The requests lasted lengthier amounts of time before quieting from satiation.

NEED. DEMANDS. F-U-L-F-I-L-L-M-E-N-T.

Only to start up again before he had enough time to refuel. Each task took tremendous physical and mental exertion.

NEED. D-E-M-A-N-D-S. F-U-L-F-I-L-L-M-E-N-T.

His adrenaline level exploded at every turn, but he couldn't forget the simple fact: He was close. So close to reaching his destiny he could almost taste the majesty of his throne. Which meant he couldn't give up.

Eventually, he would relinquish his body to rest, and then start the cycle going again and again.

After filling himself up with his donuts, he used the men's room. Before leaving the stall, he remembered to leave behind his mark, and promptly jerked off atop the tan tile floor, remembering his most recent murder folly in detail to get him hot and hard.

Twenty minutes later in the Toro again, he pulled out onto the road, refueled and ready for some action.

The dose of sugar gave him a second wind, and he pondered over his next move.

"So, Crater, ol' buddy, what will you have me do next?" he asked aloud.

The voice inside was silent as if thinking over its response.

He sped ahead and began to form his own sick, deranged version of a nonsense nursery rhyme tune, filling the quiet void.

"Life's a bitch, and then she dies,

Stick a needle in her eyes,

No one has to ever know,

Eenie-meenie-miney-mo."

Whoop-de-doo!

Emilio was in the best of spirits.

***

Hours later, upon waking up from her coma, she found herself in a hazy world, where everything was indistinct and unclear. Her hearing was muted. The sound of the television was a static buzz. Her sight was fuzzy. The bright sunlight shining through the window stung her weary eyes. Her body and muscles felt numb. She tried to lift her arm but couldn't summon the strength from within to function properly.

She knew her movements would eventually return but wished she didn't need to wait for them to decide when they'd do it. She cursed her stiff bones and muscles for not responding to what her brain instructed.

She couldn't remember what happened to her, why she was here. She looked over to see a sleeping man beside her and immediately recognized his face, but not how he fit into her life. She struggled to discipline her thinking, certain her memory would slowly return given time and if she concentrated hard enough.

The name suddenly popped into her head.

His name is Kyran Cornell.

Why does it ring a bell?

Seconds ticked by.

He's a movie actor.

Do I know him personally? I must.

With the beginning of a headache coming on, she could think of nothing else. Her confidence suddenly disappeared and was replaced with fear. She couldn't recall another thing. Her head pounded incessantly.

She decided to focus her concentration on movement instead and managed to raise her hand an inch. Then two. She was excited by her progress. The rustling of the crisp sheets was sufficient to make the man seated beside her suddenly jerk from his slumber and sit up erect. He turned, looking directly into her face. He seemed astonished.

"H-Hello," she said. Her speech was slurred. Her eyes felt tired.

"Thirsty," she managed to mutter. "P-Please."

He rushed to pour some water and held it to her lips to drink, allowing her to take a little at a time in order to prevent her from choking.

"I can understand why. It's been a week since you've had anything to drink or solid food to eat," he said, excitement clear in his voice.

The two looked at one another and laughed. She stared at him intensely.

"Feel better?" he asked.

She nodded, taking her eyes from him. She pretended to survey the room, saying nothing further.

"I'm glad," he continued. "I was going nuts trying to rouse you. It was pretty tough for a while, you know?"

He acted fidgety and nervous, as if he were a young boy talking with a girl he liked for the very first time. Taking a Styrofoam cup off the serving table, he poured himself a cup of ice water, the ice chuckling as it hit the side of the cup.

She smiled demurely.

"I was tempted to stay asleep so I could hear the rest of the Ingalls' saga," she said in a parched, dry voice, speaking with difficulty, her eyes closed. "But then again, I already know how it ends from the television show. I used to watch it all the time when I was a kid."

It was the longest sentence she managed so far.

"You heard me?"

"Mmm-hmm." She looked up again.

"Everything?" He seemed stunned.

"Everything."

There was a moment of uncomfortable silence. She slowly and haphazardly picked up the cup and finished off the remaining water.

"Are you comfortable?" he asked, sipping his water slowly.

"No. Not very." She smiled a smile to melt someone's heart.

"I'm sorry about that," he said deeply and sincerely. "I hope you're well enough for conversation though, because there's much I want to ask you."

***

Thirty minutes later, they were no further along than they were earlier. Kyran thought he might have to dive in and say what he had to say. He was deathly afraid she'd tell him he was out of his mind, and to get the hell out of her room.

He chewed noisily and nervously on the ice cubes in his cup.

What I wouldn't do for a cigarette right now, he thought.

He would've popped one into his mouth if not for the hospital rules.

God, there's so much to ask her, but I don't know where to start.

His mind was a jumble of fragmented sentences.

Have you been dreaming of me?

Have you been trying to contact me?

Did you visit me?

Why me?

He was afraid he'd approach the situation incorrectly and risk destroying any chance he might have with her. It was imperative he broach the discussion with discretion so as not to sound like a disturbed, demented psychopath.

Get it over with.

Now.

He hesitated, then decided to go ahead. Breathless, he paused, but before he could get a word out of his mouth, she broke the uncomfortable silence between them first.

She was looking down. It seemed she was at a loss for words herself, but then she lifted her head.

"I know who you are, but I don't know why you're here with me now."

"Oh, Jesus," he said, his optimism destroyed. His voice dropped. "You're kidding me, right?"

She shook her head in response. The look on her face revealed she was clearly puzzled.

"I thought finally the time arrived I would understand everything," he said. "Who are you?" he whispered before he was able to stop himself.

She was silent, biting her lip.

"You don't know, do you?" She stared blankly. Kyran couldn't believe it. When was this crazy, farfetched horror scene going to end?"

"I'm sorry," was all she could mutter, her eyes registering confusion.

"It's not your fault," he said enthusiastically, touched by the sense of loneliness that came through her words. "Don't worry. Give it time. I'm sure it'll come back to you eventually."

He squeezed her hand, and she looked helplessly at him, her eyes imploring him for answers, an explanation for what was happening.

"I hope so," she responded, sounding optimistic. "How do I know you?"

"Personally, we've never known one another. I would assume you've seen me in the movies I've been in. I'm sure this is how I initially became a part of your life, but somewhere along the line it became bit more intricate than that."

He wasn't sure how to go about explaining himself. He wasn't' certain how she'd react to the news, and he didn't want to upset her too much in her condition.

"Do you remember paying me a visit?"

He didn't even wait or a response. It was clear enough she couldn't recall anything other than his name.

"A week ago," he continued, "You paid me some kind of spiritual visit in my New York apartment. Before that, you were a part of a dream I've been having for the last three years running. Each night you and I were in the same beautiful dream together. I never knew who you were, but I felt somehow linked to you.

"I didn't make the connection between everything until your visit. Then, I assumed somehow you were telepathically sending me The Dream all along. I'm still not certain my assumption is correct, and, I was hoping you could clear it up for me."

"Just prior to your visit, The Dream took a dramatic turn for the worst. Suddenly, it wasn't beautiful anymore, but threatening. You were in extreme danger and in need of my help, but no matter how hard I tried to reach you, I always failed."

"When you visited me, you spoke my name and said Middlebury, Vermont. Then you vanished. Do you remember any of this at all?"

She shrugged.

"On the hunch you were trying to tell me where I could find you, I got in my car and drove out there. You have to understand, by that point, I was emotionally distressed and not in a normal state of mind."

"You did all that for me?" she asked quietly.

"For you *and* for me. I had to. You've become an intricate part of my life, and I desperately needed some answers."

He realized his response was vague and blunt, but he wasn't ready to delve deeper into the emotions involved.

"I'm sorry I can't give the answers to you," she sounded like she felt badly about the trouble he went through to help her. "I appreciate all you've done. I don't know how to thank you—all the time you've spent by my bedside. You don't have to do that, and it means a great deal to me."

"I did it because I wanted to," he said, spoken with genuine emotion. "I'm glad I was able to find yo9u, and I will remain at your side to help you through it all if that's what you'd like. Somehow, some way, we're going to find out who you are, but I think I've given you more than enough to think about for the time being. The good doctor is going to be anxious to hear you're finally awake. So, I'll go inform the head nurse and leave you until tomorrow. Okay?"

He gave her hand another reassuring squeeze.

"Okay and thanks," she said.

Before closing the door, he stuck his head back in to say, "Don't worry. Everything will be fine. Give it time. I'm sure you'll remember."

***

After leaving The Woman he now referred to as Jane to allow her some privacy, Kyran pondered over the present predicament. He hoped the use of the name, Jane Doe, would be temporary and not a long-lasting thing, and soon they would know her real identity.

In the short while they spent together, Kyran found she was a timid, but sincere woman who spoke more expressively with her eyes and motions than through words. She did it without even realizing it, and he was able to understand more about her simply by watching her. This helped immensely in dealing with the awkwardness of their situation.

He hadn't really wanted to leave her, but he needed to get some rest of his own. Their long-awaited conversation took a toll on them both. He decided to go directly to the Middlebury Inn and hit the hay.

He sluggishly walked into his room, barely making it to the bed. He didn't even pause to remove his clothing. He couldn't tolerate the thought of having to take them off, but simply plopped onto the bed, resting his head in the softness of the pillow.

It seemed everything from the last three years piled into this one single day, drawing every bit of strength he had remaining.

The reality that it started three years earlier with The Dream, and not merely with the search for The Woman, was overwhelming. He was carrying the weight of its perplexity on his shoulders the entire time, and it only got worse and worse. He became so deeply and mentally distraught by it all.

At first there was the question of why it was happening. Was he going crazy or lacking something vital in his life?

Then, it was The Dream turned Nightmare, followed by The Woman's outlandish, ghostly visit, and then his quest to find this Woman at the center of it all. Although he regained his sanity when finding her, he still didn't have the answer to why. It was only made harder with her being comatose.

Now, upon her waking, he immediately presumed the answers would flow freely, and life would be grand from then on. But he was wrong. She lost her memory, and he would've waited yet again until she got it back to get i8answers he so desperately desired. Hopefully.

When would it end? Would it ever?

As he lay there, falling deeper and deeper into the throes of sleep, he became angry at fate. Why did it have to be so complicated? The plushness of the feather pillow and blanket gave him no consolation. He rolled over, tossing and turning, something he was doing a lot of lately.

He knew getting so angry and upset over something he had no control of was silly and his anger slowly dissipated. He looked to the brighter side of things, like locating The Woman and finally having her in his life, possibly his future.

Take it one day at a time, and everything will be fine.

Kyran tried following the advice he gave Jane before leaving her. Yet, he couldn't help but worry.

How long would it take? Was she still in any danger from whomever it was who hurt her in the first place? His last thought before falling into a deep slumber was that there was no choice but to wait it out and see.

He was asleep for a good half hour when the telephone rang. He came out of his sleep with great difficulty, almost hesitating before picking it up, but quickly thinking better of it. Prying his eye open, he reached for the phone.

It was Dr. Winthrop.

"I apologize for calling at such a late hour, but I thought you'd be interested in the results of the tests made on Jane," he said.

"Yes, of course," Kyran responded. He quietly listened, occasionally interjecting with a brief *yes* to let the doctor know he was awake and listening.

"We just completed a number of tests on her which we were unable to do while she was comatose."

"Fortunately, she is merely suffering from a mild form of amnesia called selective amnesia. Although she has total loss of her personal memories, she hasn't lost the ability to utilize other faculties such as her educational skills.

"An easy way of explaining it would be if you compared the brain to a rechargeable battery. As the battery is used, it weakens and requires recharging. Although it hasn't lost its juice entirely, it still functions to a certain capacity, utilizing what energy it does have. Because it isn't working to full capacity, it's selective in the amount of output it offers.

"The brain undergoes a similar change. When the body is comatose, it loses much of its energy, focusing its attention on one main goal: Life. When the patient awakens, they sometimes will suffer from amnesia, because there isn't enough juice going into the mainframe component of the brain. Therefore, the brain is selective in what the patient can or can't do. Now that life has been sustained, its new goal is a function of getting by or managing. As the body regenerates itself, other unnecessary survival memories come back."

"Although the personal information is a total blank, I'm confident she'll recover it, given time. Considering the ramifications of the injuries she sustained to date, she survived it all when I had no reason to believe she would. She could very well have died, but she didn't. The coma implied the possibility of brain damage, and yet I see no implications of that whatsoever, merely amnesia, something which is quite common in coma patients."

"The police have already written down their description of her and will continue to try and find out who she is. I'm sure as time goes on, and she reads or watches television, something will trigger a memory. Of course, if the police discover her identity first, we won't have to wait long to find out who she is anyway. Identity alone can bring memory back, slower with some people than with others."

"I think you're doing a wonderful thing, Mr. Cornell. Not many people fall into a situation as this and stay put."

After hanging up with Dr. Winthrop, Kyran was too preoccupied with the conversation they had and was unable to get to sleep. He lay in bed thinking about Jane Doe and about what the good doctor would really think of him if he knew the sordid details. He'd probably think he was a looney. Thank goodness he was able to win his confidence over thus far.

After explaining to Jane in the best way he could the part he played in the events of their bizarre union, he failed to mention the extent of his own feelings for her which initially prompted his motives. Revealing only the basics, he purposely left out the part about his intense emotional attachment, because he felt it was necessary to forestall the knowledge until she had time to think, remember, and finally discern her own emotions in return. Although he felt immeasurably connected to her, intertwined to her mentally like an electrical current surging through a power line, he couldn't fool himself into believing the feeling might be reciprocated.

Conversation and communication began with difficulty but had gradually advanced to a stage where talking came easily and comfortably. He was unable to learn any factual information on her personally, but he clearly saw she was quiet, kind, patient, and trustworthy. Although he was unsure whether it was simply a personality trait of hers or not, he was confident he played a big part in the reason for her reacting that way even though she suffered, was still suffering, from a harrowing ordeal. He hoped it was a sign that things would only get better, eventually helping her remember her past and identity.

He just laid back down on his pillow when the phone rang again. This time it was Chief Beckham.

"We know who she is," he said firmly. "And we'll be telling her in the morning."

Kyran snapped up to attention. He couldn't believe it was true. His prayers were answered. He was confused, not sure whether to be happy or sad. They were so quick about it, but the fact remained that although the police knew who she was, she still had no recollection. Kyran would keep his promise to her and be there for her if she wanted him to. He had a gut feeling they were on their way to recovery. Lady luck was finally on their side.

He spoke a little longer with Chief Beckham and then hung up. He leaned back and closed his eyes. Now he could finally relax and sleep without fear.

Kyran summoned up a white-clouded dream of softness where stars filled a broad sky. In its midst, he lovingly reached out his hands to

The Woman, Victoria Sheldon, and guided her deep into the plushness of his heartfelt embrace.

Alone in her room, she closed her eyes and forced herself to concentrate once again on recalling her memories. She tried and tried, squeezing her eyelids tighter together but saw nothing but vivid darkness, as if she were looking directly into a movie screen gone entirely black.

The mere thought it could remain that way, a darkened screen in her mind, for the rest of her life was frightening. She might as well have been dead for all that it mattered.

Knowing about this dream for which she had no recollection bothered her tremendously. Was she responsible for Kyran having it in the first place? No matter how hard she tried, she couldn't steer away from this line of thinking.

Suddenly, the blackened screen inside her head revealed a vision of Kyran taking form. It continued until it totally shaped itself into precise clarity. She was in a place that could only have been heaven, because stars surrounded them in a world of white and silver wonder. The stars shined brightly, glimmering.

The sight of Kyran's smiling eyes soothed her, filling her body and mind with warmth, love and security. Subconsciously, she understood if Kyran were the only thing she would ever have again, she could accept it and go on, content with his support and companionship. As long as he was at her side, she could somehow survive. Although she wasn't certain he felt the same way, she somehow sensed he did; an unspoken truth and understanding. They belonged together.

She was so terribly grateful for him. Where would she be now without him? Who was she? Was someone else looking for her? If so, why didn't she remember them?

She fell deeper and deeper into thought. On the screen in her mind, she noticed Kyran reaching an outstretched hand in her direction. She put hers out to take his and relaxed in the comfort of his familiar embrace.

Why is it familiar?

She didn't know, but she considered it a gracious gift, nonetheless.

A gift from God.

Without it, she would have no will to live. She bowed her head, praying silently.

***

Emilio had been steadily on the move for almost a week since the incident with the bitch got away, and Crater tortured his mind endlessly.

IS SHE ALIVE? DID SHE GET AWAY?

If so, where is she?

Is she dead?

Is she alive?

Is she dead?

Is she A L I V E?

He desperately wanted to hear the latter and shut Crater up for good. The whole event would be put to rest. He never left loose ends behind, and it nagged at him repeatedly.

He'd traded cars many times over and left many dead along the way. In order to keep cops off his trail, he dumped them and buried them where no one would find them.

He realized his murder rampage induced in him an urgent need to release his sex, and a hand job wasn't going to do the trick. But luck seemed to be heavy on his side.

Driving along the interstate, he picked up a bimbo hitchhiker. She looked about nineteen or twenty years old, twenty-one at the most, and was clearly heavily addicted to drugs.

After picking her up and promising her some dope, she agreed to stop with him at a motel.

Emilio knew it would take little or nothing to get her wasted, but he didn't plan on bargaining anymore anyway. He'd take what he wanted no matter what she felt about it. The second she set foot in the car she was his to do with what he pleased. It was his fate.

Along the way, he stopped at a QuikChek twenty-four hour store and picked up two six packs of Miller, a couple of ham and cheese sandwiches, and potato chips. He was tempted to make it a robbery and waste the scrawny cashier but decided against it.

Too risky.

It was imperative to keep a low profile. He couldn't afford to draw unwanted attention to himself. He was already taking a chance with the chick, but needs took priority, and he was sure no one witnessed him picking her up.

He took a little extra time out to buy drugs without difficulty in finding a location for the purchase. He was knowledgeable in this type of search. Every town had a bad side, even small towns. All you needed was a good eye to find them. He was excited about treating himself to a sizable dose of crack come dessert time.

He took a room at The Appalachian Motel, a small dive in the heart of Pennsylvania.

Sex first. Sleep next. He needed to get some sleep, but he had to get his priorities straight.

MUST. SET. PRIORITIES.

The room was shoddy and small. Painted in a flat blue, it was equipped only with a tiny television set, twin bed, and functional abode. He had a choice between a room with a phone or a room with a T.V. and opted for one with a screen. Since being on the run, he made it a habit to tune into all the news broadcasts, making sure none contained stories related to him.

They weren't even in the room two minutes before the bimbo was into the stash of crack. Emilio figured he'd let her do some to get her going. He left her alone and went over to the tiny television set and flicked it on to the local news station. The reception wasn't the greatest, but it was visible and audible enough to suffice. The weatherman was conveying the upcoming weather forecast.

Uninterested, Emilio ignored the set for the time being, and proceeded to throw the paper bag filled with the groceries onto the bed, along with his satchel bag which contained the few personal items he had accumulated, and went into the john to take a piss.

The rust-encrusted waterspout of the sink dripped water in steady *kurplop* sounds. He grabbed his throbbing penis in his hand. While he whizzed, he thought about the time when he'd finally accomplish his destiny. He understood it was close at hand. Then, he wouldn't have to deal with a shitbox place like this, or any two-bit bimbos either.

When he came out, the bimbo was totally out of it, having succumbed to the effects of the drug. Her head was lolling from side to side as she hummed a half-assed version of a Jason Mraz tune, her eyelids flickering up and down in slow motion.

Emilio looked over at the T.V. set and saw it was a commercial. Jessica Simpson, has-been singer, was wearing a sexy, tight-fitting dress and informing America she loved her body no matter what shape, but she liked the shape she was in now even more because of Weight Watchers.

WE HEARD IT FROM YOU FIRST, BABE, Crater exclaimed.

"Fucking-A," Emilio announced, while chomping on a sandwich. He'd rather fuck on a full stomach.

He was halfway through his third beer and second ham sandwich when a news story caught his attention. There was a photo up on the screen.

"Victoria Sheldon, wife of Adam Sheldon, CEO of..." the balding newscaster was saying.

Emilio didn't hear the words.

"Mr. Sheldon filed a missing person's report after his wife failed..."

All he could think about was the picture of the woman on the screen behind his shiny head. It was her. The bitch.

She's alive?

Malevolence permeated from within his blank stare. His sweat glands suddenly released an odor of an evil and rotting stench like a lingering faint, sick smell of infection. Rage and revenge inextricably controlled him.

Disrespectful, he declared. *How dare she?*

He quickly turned to look and see if the bimbo was listening in on the news, as well. She was pretty far gone but had managed to undo her jeans and slide them off, throwing them onto the floor, leaving on only her panties. She was working her finger in between her legs; painstakingly stroking herself.

Emilio, satisfied, turned his attention back to the broadcast.

"The story became even more mysterious after the charred remains of Mrs. Sheldon's car were discovered in Layton, New Jersey possibly linking her with the murder of a Layton resident, Lyle Mitchum, whose body..."

Victoria Sheldon.

Although Emilio could've gotten that information himself simply by looking at her driver's license inside the bag she inadvertently left behind after jumping from the car, he hadn't bothered to, because he was so sure she'd end up dead. They always did.

WE NEVER LEAVE BEHIND LOOSE ENDS, Crater reminded him. *YOU FUCKED UP LIKE I FIGURED YOU WOULD!*

Emilio was madder than hell. *Luck can't be running out. It can't.*

How could she have survived? He was stifling with rage and found himself pounding his fist into the floor. Every slam left him with a tremendous feeling of renewed power, invigorated.

"...deepens even further with the discovery of a hospitalized Victoria Sheldon in Middlebury, Vermont where, after coming out of a coma, she is suffering from amnesia and has no recollection of the ill-fated night of her disappearance. Mrs. Sheldon will return to her home in Vernon, New Jersey and undergo therapy in order to help her regain her memory. In the meantime, police are working on..."

Suffering from amnesia, huh? Maybe it's not so bad after all, but how the hell did she end up in Vermont?

"Fucking slut," he mumbled.

Was she running away from him, or was she running away from something else? Maybe she was lying about the amnesia. Or, maybe it was a trick on the cops' part. It seemed suspicious, but nobody was smart enough to pull one on him! He was almost certain the news left out a very important detail. Nevertheless, he'd find out sooner or later.

For now, she was returning home, and Emilio wasn't taking any chances on her pointing the finger at him. He would outsmart them all and take care of unfinished business.

He was almost certain, as well, that she hadn't mentioned him yet. Otherwise, thanks to his reputation to date, his picture would've been plastered all over national T.V. After all, he was no spring chicken. He was a wanted man, a *very* wanted man. If she told the police, and they discovered who her assailant was, the authorities would've taken full advantage of the broadcasting system and the eye of the public to apprehend his ass. But she still posed an immediate threat to his cover, and he needed to dispose of her as soon as possible.

He was determined, adamant to find her, exterminate her.

So, determined.

Ever so determined.

Search. Find. Kill.

He wanted to peel away her pretty face, pluck out her smiling eyes.

Although insanity took root within the confines of Emilio's brain long ago, in the brief passage of days it grew to full proportion. In this one crazed moment, the transformation took its final turn.

Emilio and Crater *became* one in the same, no longer separate in thinking. The Emilio side of his mind snapped, vaporized. Crater, the stronger of the two minds, took over, assuming total control. Although his outward appearance depicted the everyday Emilio of before, his mind and function zone became that of his Crater entity, and Crater wanted Victoria Sheldon dead.

All along, Emilio Rodriguez believed himself to be the brains behind the operation, the stronger of the two minds, but in truth, Crater always been the real one in charge. Whatever self-control Emilio sustained to date totally deteriorated. It ripped away until none remained.

The blatant, angry emotions piled up by the second until an intense hunger prevailed. His hunger pang for blood knotted his stomach with pain more terrible than any he had ever imagined. The knot tightened with every second, clenching and squeezing violently as if punishing him for not supplying the total nourishment it demanded. He was starving, starving for blood, and the only answer to his starvation would be found with Victoria Sheldon.

His hatred of the bitch was overwhelming, and his need to destroy her for causing him problems built into a frenzied obsession. For whatever crazed reason, killing her became the most important focus of his mission. Taking revenge on her, the ultimate purpose of his existence.

The very thought of her brought forth a rage so intense that Crater sent his hand crashing through the television screen.

Crater's anger momentarily subsided when he noticed the pieces of shredded glass lying beneath the ruined screen. Smoke wafted above the top. Blood dripped from a cut received from his perilous action. Somehow pain evaded him, and he was exhilarated. For a time, he stared at the broken screen. The giant hole in the monitor looked much like a mouth frozen in a silent scream. When he finally focused his mind and thoughts back to reality, he realized the bimbo was laughing. He turned and glared at her.

She put a hand over her mouth to hide the grin, but the developing chuckle discharged, nonetheless. Behind her white-skinned palm, she giggled uncontrollably.

"You think it's funny, slut?" Crater shrieked through clenched teeth, his voice bristling, his eyes flashing dangerously.

She immediately stifled herself and became frightened by the look in his eyes.

"N-No," she managed to say.

An uneasy look came into her eyes. She lowered them and turned away.

Need. Demanded. Fulfillment.

"What the fuck's so funny?" he asked, leaping to his feet and rushing over to her, repeatedly slapping her upside the head. "Huh? What the *fuck* is so funny?"

Need. Demands. Fulfillment.

"Ah-h-h-h," she cried, putting her arms up to shield herself. She attempted to get up and run, but Crater forced her down with harder blows. He continued to beat her, allowing the fury within him to take over.

"I'll teach you to fucking laugh at me, you lousy slut."

He was enraged and engrossed in releasing it. Blood dripped from open wounds. He broke her nose. Her eyes were bloody and swollen shut. Luckily for her, she was knocked out completely. When his rage was satiated, he stopped to check if she was breathing. She was. The excitement of the event ignited his manhood. It was popping inside his jeans. He unzipped them and took it out.

His Need. Demanded. Fulfillment.

It was hard and red and ready for action.

He took her roughly, relieving himself in a wild frenzy. She woke up just as he came, and she managed a muffled scream. Crater laughed. Finally spent, he whipped out his blade and cut her throat.

His Need. Demanded. Fulfillment.

To satisfy the remaining urge within him, he cut off her nipples and fingers; wiping the red goo of her insides from his fingers onto the white sheets beneath them.

Coming out of his self-induced trance-like state, he noticed he left behind bloodied sheets and pillowcases and her body spread across the blood-drenched surface.

She won't be playing with herself no more, he thought to himself, snickering, capering with insane pride.

Crater decided he was one step nearer to his psychological nemesis—all a part of his destiny. It was his way of making a disgusting act seem logical. He was profoundly thrilled by the act of violence he just committed, and his Need was thoroughly satisfied. This Need, in part, arose from the belief he was different. He had a special purpose in life.

He lay down on the floor beside the broken T.V. set, in the center of puddles of blood, cushioning his crumbled jacket under his head.

Yes. He was momentarily satiated and glad for it.

As he lay there, his mind wandered.

Was it a sign of his God-like destiny?

Was something proclaiming him untouchable, indomitable, invincible?

He lay still, devising it all out in his head; carefully organizing every detail, getting more and more excited by the minute at the prospect. Destiny would prevail.

Search. Find. Kill.

Waste her.

Roll around in the pool of her blood.

Swim in an ocean among the waves.

Smother in the smoothness of its embrace.

He waconsus left lingering over his thoughts and plans. He smiled in the darkness, uncannily resembling an ugly Gremlin. His lungs bristled with energy and excitement. His lips were peeled back in a maniacal grin revealing teeth yellowed by tobacco. Drool ran down his chin. It was more than he could do to contain himself.

He smiled wider.

Time to get some z's, he thought. He drifted into a sleep filled with dreams of dismembered body parts, and the victim's face was Victoria Sheldon's. Crater slept like a thoroughly pacified baby.

***

At the precise time Crater was committing his insane act of murder, Victoria Sheldon was returning to her home. The house was a stranger to her as much as the man who stood before her. She was both frightened and confused. She was surprised at the sharpness of her displeasure at seeing Adam. Maybe it was the fact he had allowed Kyran to bring her home rather than coming for her himself. Or was it possible her feelings stemmed from something in the past she was repressing, something hidden in the memory she couldn't recall? She swallowed hard to keep from crying.

When Chief Beckham came in early that morning to tell her about what he considered to be good news, she thought she would die. Finding out her name was one thing but finding out she was married had been another. Her whole hope for the future crumbled in one second. She felt guilty feeling the way she did, but she assumed she was single and unattached. She was wrong, and now her hopes for a future with Kyran were dashed.

The drive home was long and tedious. Kyran, in a gesture of politeness, offered to bring her home to Vernon, New Jersey after Adam made no attempt to do so himself. Their departure and farewell were brief but friendly; difficult under the circumstances of the recent development of their friendship.

As she stood with her back to the bay window, she stared at the sharp features in her husband's face, searching for a tiny bit of recollection to no avail. She felt awkward, and she assumed he did, as well. She summoned every last bit of energy, reaching deep within herself to make the effort to reach and accept his outstretched hand.

She didn't know him. How else was she supposed to react? Her emotions were normal given the situation.

"It's good to see you," he said formally.

Her voice was constrained. After accepting his hand and a brief hug, she retreated as far away from him as she could without appearing rude, uncomfortably observing the room's décor, bluntly ignoring his prying eyes.

She was embarrassed. Something wasn't right. Although she couldn't remember this man, her husband, she sensed something odd in his demeanor, as if he hoped to hide something from her memory, or at least hoped she wouldn't recall it herself. It might simply be her imagination, and probably he didn't know how to react himself to being thrust into such a bizarre situation.

She wished she understood the weird feeling she had, but she shrugged it off to the inexplicable events which led to her amnesia. After all, how as she supposed to act? If the roles were reversed, how would she handle it?

Her mind was empty of memories. That wasn't his fault. She had to be strong for them both. She needed to make herself remember this man took the same marital oath as she did, to love, honor and cherish through the worst of situations. Wasn't this that kind of deal? He was obviously acting in the best way he knew how. Although his eyes appeared contemptuous, his voice said something else.

She forced herself to draw closer to him. She realized she was being rude to him, and wanted to make up for her actions, but didn't quite know how. She feigned exhaustion.

"I'm sorry, Adam," she said quietly. "I'm very tired and overwhelmed. If you don't mind, I'd like to start over again in the morning. I hope you understand."

"Certainly, Darling," he responded irritably with a slight frown.

She noticed the muscles in his neck tightening.

"Of course, I understand. I've made up the guestroom, and I'll sleep in there until you feel ready to accept me into your bed again. It's going to be a long, hard road, Victoria, but I'm confident we will be able to survive."

She nodded. Survive? Hadn't she done enough of that already? When would it all end? It was awful him being so kind, and all she could think of was Kyran and the hurt look on his face when he left her. What about Adam's feelings?

"I'll get my things," he continued somewhat sharply. "I'll see you first thing in the morning, and we can talk at breakfast."

He walked over to her, brushing a kiss lightly on her cheek.

Victoria unconsciously flinched and was immediately embarrassed by her reaction and the look of rejection clearly imprinted on his face.

"Thank you, Adam," she said. "I p-promise to be a d-different person in the morning."

"Good night, Victoria," he answered tonelessly.

He pulled the door open and walked slowly out of the room without looking back, leaving her to prepare things for herself.

Chapter Eight

Going Home

Victoria was sitting down to eat when she heard the doorbell ring. She put her fork aside, and went to answer the door, almost forgetting which direction to head. She opened it to find Kyran standing there.

"I'm sorry for coming without calling first," he said.

"It's okay," she said, scanning the yard. "Come in. I was about to eat something. Are you hungry?"

"No," he said. "Thanks anyway."

He followed her into the kitchen. On the table, a plate consisting of salad, croutons, and a variety of cut-up cold cuts sat untouched. A glass filled with water stood beside it.

She suddenly got an extra dose of nervous energy, and paced frenetically around the room, moving dishes from one spot to another, fussily fiddling with the dishrag, nervously wiping down the countertop.

Kyran quickly removed his jacket and folded it over a chair. He sat down, and lit up a cigarette, immediately thinking better of it and snuffing it out. Victoria cautiously pulled back the kitchen curtain and snuck a peek out at the driveway. She wanted to make certain Adam was nowhere in sight. If he knew Kyran were here, he'd be hurt and upset. After all, they were trying to save their marriage, weren't they?

She wasn't about to admit to Kyran that she and Adam made hardly any progress at all. Even though she had been home for two full days, she saw very little of Adam. She wallowed away, hour after hour, watching television and thinking. Starting from early morning on, it was Maury Povich from nine until eleven, a break from the talk shows with Matlock repeats at eleven, but back to them again at twelve with whichever one she could find by browsing the channels. Then from one until five, while preparing dinner and setting the table, she listened in on whatever repeat came in on the Bravo channel. She couldn't get herself to do much else. It was a thrilling two days back home.

"Do you think that maybe we can go somewhere else to talk, Kyran? I'm very nervous about Adam coming home and finding you here. You know you're sort of a sore spot with him, and we haven't had much time or privacy to sort things out with each other first."

She saw the hurt expression on Kyran's face.

"It seems like every other minute the telephone or the doorbell rings with news people wanting an update on the story. We haven't had appropriate time to sort things out between us. Besides, it's not fair to him."

She bit her lip nervously.

"He still can't understand why you spent so much time at the hospital with me when it should've been him."

She knew this wasn't true at all. In fact, Adam hadn't mentioned it once. It was merely the effects of her own guilty feelings. Although he hadn't brought it up, the coldness between the two of them made her feel ill about her feelings for Kyran, and the feelings she had toward Adam that she couldn't quite understand, because of the memory loss.

"He should be happy at least someone was with you," Kyran said in a voice rigid with anger which suddenly dissipated at the sight of Victoria's forlorn appearance. "I'm sorry," he whispered and nodded in agreement with her. "I understand. We can go for a drive, stop at a park or someplace else. Why don't you leave him a note, and you can explain things later."

"Thanks. I'll only be a minute," she said, and left him in the kitchen while she went for her jacket. She desperately wanted to avoid any further conversation about her time in the hospital. They both knew full well what his reasons for being there were. She missed him just as badly.

She came back a short time later with her jacket hanging over her arm, opened a drawer, and pulled out a pad and pen.

Kyran stood up.

"You don't have to do this if you don't want to. It was wrong of me to come knowing the way the situation is and all. I have to admit my motives for coming are purely selfish," he said as he helped her on with her jacket.

"No, it's perfectly all right," she said. "Honestly, I've missed you tremendously. Adam is a stranger to me where you're not. He's going to have to accept our friendship sooner or later."

They both looked away from one another at her mention of the word friendship.

"Things have been difficult," she added.

She passed the door to him. They remained in the threshold of the doorway, momentarily gazing at each other before heading on out to his car parked in the driveway.

"Anything come back to you memory-wise?" he asked as they got into the car.

"Absolute zilch," she said. "I'm beginning to wonder if it ever will. I can't seem to remember even the simplest things. That's why it's so hard for Adam to accept the fact that I remembered you."

Even though Adam hadn't brought up that question either, it was one that stuck in her mind constantly. Of course, it could be the fact that Kyran was a well-known public figure, but it didn't give light to the reasons for his dream and her ever insistent presence in it. And, then there was the incident of her paying him an out-of-body visit. Was it that her life was so miserable before that Kyran could make such a profound difference in her life as to induce such actions and control such emotions? She wasn't sure.

Things were clearly not perfect between her and Adam. That much was obvious. But he wasn't feeding any information into it either. In truth, he wasn't any help at all. She needed to piece things together on her own and became certain there was a problem, but she was unsure whether it was due to her illness or something that was there all along—even before she lost her memory. She hoped time would reveal the truth.

"Why remember you and nothing else?" she repeated.

Her question dampened the mood even more. She knew, without his even telling her, the reason lay in the special connection between the two of them, something she obviously lacked with Adam.

"I see your point," he said, as he pulled out of the drive and rode down the street.

He looked away, distracted. It was beginning to get dark out, and Kyran flicked on his headlights. They passed by the local movie theater displaying the week's showing of Kyran's new movie, shining brightly on the billboard in white, neon lights.

For several moments, the conversation was stagnant. They, they were both quiet, each thinking of their predicament or maybe just about each other.

Victoria thought being so close to him wasn't a good idea. It certainly wasn't easy. She wondered what Kyran was thinking about and hoped he wasn't lingering on the issue of their relationship, because it would only force the conversation further, and she couldn't handle it.

She smelled a hint of cologne, and it smelled great; sexy. She hoped to get out into the fresh air where she could get away from its tempting lure.

"Why don't you pull up over there on the right," she said, pointing in the direction of a lit-up area where a fountain stood with a finely carved wartime statue erected in the center of the pluming water. She was biting the inside of her mouth. This was a sign she was working out something in her head about what she wanted to tell him and what she wanted to leave out for fear of hurting his feelings.

It appeared to be a memorial park. Under the sweeping cover of a weeping willow tree sat picnic tables with park benches surrounding the water fountain. Metal-laced trash cans were settled here and there in several parts of the small park area. A large sign posted alongside each of them read *fifty-dollar fine for littering.*

One other car, with two teenage lovers in an embrace, was parked up ahead along the side of the curb.

The young couple got out of their car and walked arm in arm alongside the streaming water under the park's white lamplights. They stopped briefly for a lingering kiss, and then proceeded on their way.

"Adam," she began, and paused to rethink her words. *He seems nice enough. Sympathetic and supportive,* she thought. "I couldn't ask for more. After all, consider the position he's been thrust into. It's not just me here. Or, just you."

It seemed she was trying to convince herself.

"He's trying so hard to help me trigger a memory," she said hoping a few white lies wouldn't hurt any."

"Knowing you isn't helping me," she continued, realizing her words didn't come out the way she intended them to. "I don't mean to sound ungrateful, because truly I'm not. I owe you so much, Kyran. For whatever reason, I reached out to you. I remembered you when I could remember nothing else, and I don't even know why. I'm permanently indebted to you."

Damn! She still couldn't say it the way she wanted to say it.

Come out with it already!

"You're the only thing in my life that isn't a stranger," she continued. "But for now, I need to try and put my life back together. I desperately need to uncover the missing pieces. To do that, I must put you aside and out of my mind, because you're a distraction."

She paused. There was an obvious twitch to his lips, a change in his eyes as the statement took effect.

"This is insane. This man is my husband, and all I can think about is you." She started to speak further, but hesitated, then stopped.

Kyran's face started to turn a beet red. He leaned over and took her hand in his. She enjoyed touching when he touched her. The feel of him was ten times better than The Dream touches; a million times better than she ever imagined they could be. She loved the smell of him, too. She looked at his flushed cheeks and sparkling eyes and waited as he gently kissed her. She didn't resist. Although it was brief, it was loving, nonetheless.

"Please try to understand," she went on. "Maybe once I recover my memory, we can be friends. Until then, we cannot see one another. It's the best thing to do all around." She turned toward the door ready to rush from the car to wherever her feet would take her. She simply wanted out!

Kyran pulled her back. When in deep concentration, his eye squinted and his brow furrowed. His jaw had a sharpness and roughness about it.

"I'm sorry," he said.

She saw a sadness and worry in his eyes as if he realized he shouldn't have kissed her, but impulse took sudden control of his actions. She didn't regret he had done it, but it made things more difficult to accept. And, she hadn't resisted it either. As a matter of fact, she kissed him back, as well.

"I'm not sure I can do what you're asking," he continued with a natural ease to his voice. He spoke softly and intimately. "You've made a tremendous difference in my life. I want you to always remember that. I understand what you're doing, and I'll do my best to follow your wishes, but to be honest with you, it's not going to be easy. I'm only human, you know, and if I haven't mentioned it to you yet—I love you. All I ask is when you do get your life back, you reserve a spot in it for me, no matter what it is."

Victoria could scarcely listen without breaking into a fit of tears. She cherished the words he said but was reluctant to respond in any way for fear of what her response would be. At that moment, her only consolation was the sincere expression on his face. She knew she could offer no response, but was content to leave it at that, because it left an open door and not one permanently closed.

They sat there in the middle of a thick, profound silence, yet there was no mistaking the sincerity of his emotions. His commitment to her was genuine.

Victoria thought about how they were two innocent victims brought together first by fantasy then by chance. Love and fate. Maybe it was all due to the will of God. Whatever it may be, they were here together. There was no turning back. They'd need to handle the circumstances in the most morally, appropriate manner possible, and take whatever cards dealt them.

With a wordless sound of disagreement, she shook her head back and forth adamantly until she caught sight of the sadness and pain in his eyes and melted. She wanted to kiss him again, but knew it was taboo, especially considering what she just asked of him. Doing anything else would appear as though she were using him. As difficult as it was, she managed to keep her emotions in tow.

Kyran spoke in quick statements, faster and faster without hesitation, trying to convince her of the gravity of the situation. "I'll do whatever it is you ask. I don't like it, but I don't have much of a choice. First things first."

His smile was soft and agreeable, but something was clearly missing from his face. The hope. The hope for a future together. "I'll take you back home, and we can talk to Adam together. We'll explain my visit was nothing more than a friendly follow-up to your returning home. I'm not going to lie about my concern for you, and he damned well knows it. He doesn't have to know about anything we've discussed."

She didn't respond, only nodded.

Kyran started the motor, revving it lightly to warm up the engine. Then, he drove away.

***

Crater awoke at dawn ready for action. He prepared for the events ahead, and the challenge excited him. He was done by noon and sat in his room at the Warwick Inn until dark. Then he went on his way. It took him only fifteen minutes to reach his destination.

Driving slowly, Crater looked for the street signs.

Hummingbird Terrace.

Bentwood Drive.

He got the street address right off the internet. It was amazing how easy it was to locate her just by putting in her name and state. As luck would have it, they were listed. He was now following the direction given to him by the gas station attendant at the Mobil service station in town.

Bantry Court.

Lisa Drive. One more block and he'd be there.

Hickory Road.

He made the right turn and started looking for house number 11.

He parked at the foot of the street, when bright headlights suddenly shined behind him. Crater slumped in his seat waiting for it to pass. Not until then did he emerge from the car.

Dressed entirely in black, with black leather gloves to complete the ensemble, Crater approached the unlit home, his grin maniacal, the muscles in his neck taut. The smell of pine was clear and fresh in the night air, and it sickened him.

His blade, with its steel, serrated edge, glistened in the moonlight. As he grasped a tender hold of the weapon, he bellowed from within in exultation as if the mere touch alone gave him an erotic thrill.

The night wind abated slightly leaving Crater in a comfortable embrace. He dashed behind tree to tree, remaining temporarily out of sight, taking every precaution even though he was certain to hear any oncoming cars in enough time to conceal himself further.

The house was one nice sized estate among a few others in a basically undeveloped wooded area of the neighborhood. It was dark, without streetlamps to light the way, typical of the country setting and living.

Judging by the lack of lights within the house, Crater decided no one was at home—the perfect set-up for his plan.

Crouched and well-concealed behind a row of bushes at the edge of the driveway, he decided to check the garage for an alarm system, if there was one, and in case it was set. The garage was the most logical place for a keypad installation. If it was set, he'd enter and immediately disengage it. He knew how to disengage any type of alarm, because he'd done it many times before.

He hopped over a wood picket fence surrounding the house and glided up the paved driveway to the garage door with mechanical stride. He cupped his hands around his eyes and peered in through the glass pane window. He looked in the pitch blackness of the garage in search of the alarm box which would be somewhere that the homeowner would have immediate access to it. All he needed to do was look for a green light and red light to partner the green one which meant the alarm wasn't activated.

"Lucky again, Motherfucker!" Crater whispered under his breath. People were stupid enough to pay a fortune for a security system and then forget to use it. Assholes. It wouldn't have kept him out anyway. He pulled out his flashlight and brought it along in case he might need it.

Crater surveyed the garage interior.

This guy is a neat freak, he thought.

The garage was huge. Three stalls. It was supposed to be suitable for two cars and some storage but looked as though it could fit four and then some. Although not overloaded with tools and junk, it was arranged with a neat array and variety of tools and garden accessories, all aligned carefully, and labeled on a set of metal shelves going straight down the center.

There were cans of spray paint, canned paint, polyurethane, car oil, bags of garden soil, lime and grass seed. On one side of the floor lay a weed whacker, leaf blower and lawnmower with a red tank labeled *gasoline* directly next to it. A blue tank identical, but for the color, sat beside it labeled *kerosene.* Two metal ladders, one a six rung and one an extendible, hung on hooks directly above the tanks. A shiny white bicycle which appeared to be brand new, hung on a bicycle hook. Crater noticed both car stalls were empty.

Now down by one Hyundai, he chuckled gleefully, recalling the night it all began.

He realized his thoughts were straying of late, and he struggled to keep them focused on his objectives.

He would wait and hide and slip out in surprise when she got home.

Then, I'll kill her. Cut 'er good is what I'll do, his mind exclaimed. Maybe even fuck her first for the fun of it! Then, torture her! Cut off her nipples! Ram a knife down her throat! Yeah! Cut out her heart!

The idea grew more appealing by the second. Crater gasped with excitement, cutting the sound off short. He was excited so much by the prospect that he came close to peeing his pants. He focused his mind on the task at hand and proceeded with caution, tiptoeing for fear someone might hear him, even though he was certain he was alone.

He walked around the yard in search of a basement window concealed in the darkness. When he found one, he got down on his knees, scraping the gravel ground beneath him, and covered portions of it in duct tape, crossing the glass in several areas, and inaudibly broke it, allowing entry into the room below it.

After smoothing back his hair from his face and wiping away the sweat that formed on his brow and upper lip, he carefully lowered himself inside and found himself coated in velvety darkness. He lit the flashlight long enough to locate the staircase upwards. Once there, he shut it off again.

He found the upstairs doors unlocked.

Very thorough of them, he thought sarcastically, snickering under his breath.

He found himself in the darkened dining room and decided he needed to use the flashlight. He shined the flash downwards so that no one from the outside would spot it through the windows.

The room opened to French doors and was done up in southwestern décor with shades of peach and green prevailing. Pottery vases holding long stalks of rainbow-colored ting-tings decorated one corner. He walked around the table into a little sitting area where a floor lamp in sand tones, its shade opening into a wide arc and its base accented with pottery-shaped additions in pastel colors, stood beside a pastel-colored sofa. He was tempted to break something for the sheer pleasure of it but thought better of it. He couldn't afford to waste time. The hallway spirited cathedral ceilings with a skylight above it. Crater made his way up the stairwell, and silently searched the rooms one by one, looking to make sure no one inhabited them.

When he finally made his way back onto the main floor and into the kitchen, it was darker than the rest of the house, and Crater bumped into a table, knocking over a chair and glass.

"Shit!"

He was halfway into the kitchen when he heard the garage door opening, its drum-drumming lasting only seconds, stopping, then resumed again as its button was pushed to close the door back down again. Crater slipped into the hallway closet to lie in wait.

***

Adam pulled the car in and entered the house by way of the garage door. The house was enveloped in darkness—an indication

Victoria wasn't at home.

The uncaring, ungrateful wench! Adam thought to himself.

He looked around for a note, finding it on the dining room table. It read:

Unexpected visitor. Went out to diner for dessert. Be back soon.

- *Victoria*

"Unexpected visitor, huh?" Adam repeated out loud. "Unexpected, my ass! It's probably that idiot of an actor, Kyran Cornell, come to fuck her! Stupid bitch."

I better not let it get to me, he thought. *I'm no angel either. But she's not supposed to want to be with anyone else! Damn! I'll have a hefty talk with her when she gets in. I'll put a stop to this bullshit.*

He paced back and forth nervously.

There's no sense sitting around waiting for her. I don't want her thinking I'm sulking my bleeding heart out. Too bad Lina up and left so quickly. Otherwise, I woulda said, fuck it, and stayed with her for the rest of the night. It woulda been good having Victoria come home wondering about where I was!

He turned the living room lights on and worked his way to the rooms upstairs. He entered the master bedroom bath, pulling off his tie and unbuttoning his shirt.

A nice, hot luxurious bath will do me a lot of good right now, he decided.

He pulled open the cabinet, taking the container of bubble bath out. He opened it, pouring some into the Jacuzzi bathtub, and ran the water. He took the rest of his clothes off and stepped in.

Ahh, he thought. *Definitely therapeutic. Just the thing after a hard night's work.* Adam snickered under his breath. *And was it hard!*

The touch of the hot, steamy water made him take a long piss. The bubble bath water always had that effect on him. He liked the fact he could take a piss without making any effort. Someone once told him piss water was a good moisturizer for the skin. Soaking in bubbles and letting loose was almost as good as jerking off in bathwater, except he wasn't too keen on washing up in semen. As the bubbles melted into the bath water, they appeared to be a million tiny amoeba floating around in bodily fluid.

He lay back and closed his eyes, taking another small tinkle as he did so.

Mmmm, he thought. *I think I'm going to like the way things are around here from now on. I'll make it perfectly clear to Victoria how I feel about Kyran Cornell, and she will suck up to it like she always did with everything else I ever said. Yes. This is the life! How many other guys were there that could say they had their cake and ate it too? Not many, I'm sure.*

With that thought in mind, he lay back soaking and pissing to his heart's content.

***

Crater remained hidden in the closet after he heard the garage door close. He waited patiently for what seemed like hours. Footsteps stopped in front of the closet door, and Crater was prepared to kill immediately if she opened the door, although he wouldn't be too thrilled at having to do it so soon, because he really wanted to take his sweet ass time. If he had no choice, he'd do it, but Crater was confident fate would work things his way. His luck was too strong. And, as his mind screamed, *I told you so*, the footsteps left the front of the closet door and headed up the stairwell.

Patience, Crater reminded himself. He must be patient. He licked his lips in anticipation and frustration.

Patient. Patient. Patient! Patient!

He'd always had a problem with patience. Impatience and spontaneity had been the causes most responsible for him getting into trouble. They were responsible for testing his willpower to the limit, and he had many a close call because of them.

He waited for what seemed like an eternity, then quietly slid from the closet, following up the stairs in the direction of the footsteps he heard before.

Crater was quick and sly, so self-assured, confident of not being heard. It wasn't in his cards. No. Her approaching death—that was in his cards.

Gripping the handrail with extreme intensity, he treaded slowly upon the carpeted steps of the stairway to avoid making noise. He glided upwards like a cat in search of prey.

Once at the top, he heard running water and walked in that direction. Carefully scoping the area around him, he worked his way into the room, heading toward the sound of the running water.

She's taking a bath, he thought to himself. Perfecto! She'll have no way out.

Crater whipped his blade out in full view.

As he drew closer to the half-closed door, he clearly heard the hum-humming sound of a ceiling exhaust fan above and an occasional splash-splash of water as the woman repositioned herself in the tub. He was excited, his adrenaline level high. Brandishing his weapon high, he silently peered in.

It wasn't Victoria Sheldon. It was a man.

Fury erupted inside him so quickly, he almost had no time to control it. His eyes fixed on the male, glaring.

Fuck! He silently screamed his disapproval.

Be quick about it before he looks up and sees you. The man was relaxing with his eyes closed, his hand cuddling his penis.

What a fucking queer, Crater decided. *Taking a bubble bath like a prima donna! Sucker don't even know I'm here. Dispose of him!*

Thoughts were swirling in and out of his mind in tangled jumbles.

Crater moved in quickly.

***

Adam saw the attack coming only a fraction of a second before it happened, not ample time to do anything about it. One second, he sensed a presence and opened his eyes slowly, fearlessly. The next second he was overpowered and physically restrained by an unusually strong individual. Adam Sheldon never knew what hit him.

***

Crater's lips were pulled all the way back in a maniacal grin.

This is really becoming an adventure, he thought.

He looked for a decent hiding spot and found one in the huge master bedroom walk-in closet. He settled himself down, relaxing his mind, and waited.

***

Kyran and Victoria walked into the lit house slightly fearful of how Adam might react. Everything was quiet. Too quiet. Victoria gave Kyran a puzzled look and shrugged. She followed him into the kitchen, flicking on the light switch along the way.

Kyran moved around cautiously. He caught sight of her salad sitting atop the table where she left it, but her glass lay sideways, the spilled water glistening atop the table. The chair was overturned. The pad which Victoria used to writer her note to Adam sat in the middle of the puddle, soaked and no longer useable. Something was wrong. Kyran turned to look at Victoria.

"What the—" she started to say, but Kyran held up his hand to silence her.

Cold chills crawled up his spine, quickly working their way up to the nape of his neck. He stood in the middle of the floor not sure what to do with himself. He couldn't shake the impression which came so violently to him. The scene wasn't overly dramatic, but it was enough to warn Kyran something was amiss. Maybe Adam was drunk and in a fury over Victoria's absence. He didn't know the guy well enough, so he couldn't put it past him. He was always prepared for any kind of situation. If Adam was in a fury, Kyran would know how to handle it. He was increasingly nervous. Nevertheless, Kyran *knew* something was wrong. He stood immobile, listening.

Listening.

Something wasn't *right.* Kyran felt it in his bones, a sudden insecurity and sense of foreboding taking root. He felt somehow there was some connection between Victoria's accident, her memory loss, and the odd, unnatural emptiness inside the house at that moment. Trepidation filled the air like a dark cloud.

Realistically, Kyran knew his hunch was irrational, the product of the events which brought them together in the first place. But then again, those same farfetched events made anything possible, and he'd make certain to take every precaution just in case. As the old motto went, "It's better to be safe than sorry." He motioned to Victoria to follow him.

When faced with danger, Kyran's breathing became deep and hard, his chest moving fervently with every move.

Please, Lord, don't let me make a mistake, he thought to himself.

He was doing a lot of pleading and praying lately for a not-so-religious person.

Her beautiful face was lined with frustration and soft vulnerability. As far as Kyran could recall, he hadn't seen the same expression on her face except for in The Dream.

They warily looked throughout the first-floor rooms, searching them one by one haphazardly. He didn't fully believe they had anything to worry about. He suspected that the nerve ending suspicion they probably shared was due to their own personal guilt at having deceived Adam about the feelings they had for one another. Kyran's guilt stemming from the fact Victoria was a married woman, and Victoria's simply for having fallen in love with another man.

"Where do you suppose Adam could've gone?" Kyran asked. "He certainly left in a hurry. He left all the lights on in the house."

"You keep forgetting, Kyran, I don't know him, because I don't remember him," she said.

They circled back through the kitchen into the dining room, passing the basement door, relieved to have found every room empty. Maybe there wouldn't be a confrontation after all. Kyran looked over at the foyer.

"Stay here. I'll check the basement."

He walked toward the upstairs stairwell, stopped, glanced at the hallway above and listened. Moonlight glimmered in through the skylight. Confident he hadn't heard anything out of the ordinary, he proceeded down the basement stairs.

***

Upstairs in the master bedroom walk-in closet, Crater remained hidden within the confines of a corner, lying in wait for the coming of the woman, Victoria Sheldon. It couldn't be a very long wait. She should be arriving soon, and as soon as he finished her off, his deed would be complete, and no loose ends left behind. Everything would be in order, as it should've been from the start. Then, he could simply sit back and wait as his destiny unfolded around him.

***

I might as well check the upstairs, Victoria decided. She quietly walked upstairs to the hallway just outside her bedroom door, deep in thought over the current situation at hand. If not for the softness of Kyran's eyes and cheekbones, Victoria would've been frightened by his appearance.

God, I hope nothing happened, she prayed. *I hope this is all a terrible misunderstanding.* She thought the chances of that were pretty slim. *I should never have gone out with Kyran. Oh, God, please let Adam be all right. I hope he hasn't done something irrational. Is he capable of that?*

She didn't know. She cursed her memory loss vehemently. She didn't even know her own recollection of his mood swings to compare it to.

Our fears must be ridiculous, she tried convincing herself.

She couldn't believe Adam was capable of being so angry. He seemed to be a rational man who wouldn't overreact. The only logical explanation she could come up with was he accidentally bumped into the table, not realizing he'd knocked over the chair and glass. Maybe he was drunk. He'd been under a lot of stress lately, with her disappearance and subsequent discovery.

The master bedroom door was slightly ajar, light illuminating from within. Victoria hesitantly pushed it in a little too hard, making it bang into the wall behind it. She jumped, listening for any noise.

She slowly walked into the room, looking behind her every few seconds. Assured that Adam was not lurking nearby, she walked in the direction of the master bedroom's bath, from which light flickered underneath the closed door. She heard the exhaust fan running, its steady hum at work, relieving the room of any steam given off by hot water. She realized Adam must be bathing. Otherwise, the fan would've been off.

Suddenly, she was relieved, realizing they overreacted. It *was* all a silly misunderstanding after all. Adam was only bathing. He might be a bit drunk which would explain the overturned chair and glass.

"Adam?" she called. She received no answer. Frowning, she moved ahead, somewhat worried, but certain the reason he wasn't responding was because he hadn't heard her above the noise of the exhaust fan, or because he dozed off in the comfort of the warm bath water.

"Adam?" she tried again. She knocked on the door and waited.

***

Quiet. Careful not to make a sound and forewarn her. Breathing lightly.

Crater heard Victoria Sheldon calling out a man's name. Adam. He realized it must be the name of the dude he did in the bathroom.

He was ready to surprise her but decided to allow her the

pleasure of discovering the surprise he'd left for her behind the bathroom door, which would leave her too stunned to react to his impending attack upon her.

He listened, waiting for the absolute perfect moment, struggling for patience.

***

"Adam, are you in there?" Victoria asked, knocking.

He had to be! That much was obvious. She grabbed the knob now feeling a bit annoyed, turned it and pushed it inward.

Adam's bloodied, mutilated body lay in red-thickened, bubbled bathwater, most of the bubbles having already disappeared, but the few remaining reddened by the blood which flowed from his severed veins.

Victoria screamed.

***

Crater heard her speak again.

"Adam, are you in there?"

Crater slowly crawled out of his hiding place underneath suits and dresses, cautiously pushing the closet door open. He clearly saw the back of her head seconds before she pushed the bathroom door inward.

He hurried, preparing to make his move upon her.

No loose ends. Fate. Destiny.

***

The next thing Victoria knew, she was being approached by someone from behind. It all happened in a matter of seconds. She turned to see who it was, assuming it was Kyran coming after her scream. She swung around sharply, but it wasn't him.

She was frozen by the sight of him. Facing him squarely, she was paralyzed by terror, too stricken to scream again. Reason told her to plead, "Please don't hurt me." Her face suddenly paled. Her mouth was agape, but no sound escaped. Her jaw quivered. She trembled with revulsion, slowly backing away toward the master bedroom fireplace. She stared at him with a twisted expression on her face, suddenly remembering and terrified, not immediately believing. Fear and bewilderment overwhelmed her. She was so close to him she could clearly see the unspeakable rage and thirst for revenge in his gaze. Suddenly, she was struck light-headed and dizzy. Memories came sweeping back to her in a rush of fire. Within that instant, years of recollections consumed her.

The time she nearly drowned in Silver Lake if not for Uncle Paul.

The puffy jacket she'd gotten for her twelfth birthday.

Her eighteenth birthday; alone and confused, on her own.

Adam courting her. Their troubled marriage.

Her obsession and unceasing love for Kyran.

This man. *My attacker.*

The dread and fear she felt on that ill-fated evening came back in full force. Falling further and further into a deep chasm of recognition.

His eyes.

They were the same, yet somehow different.

Evil. They were deranged.

His rough abuse.

Her frenzied escape.

All her injuries.

How did he find me? The news broadcast!

Although she was relieved to have her memory back, it did nothing to help the feeling of horrified emotion she felt at recalling the events of the evening when it all began. He was responsible for what happened to her. Of course, if not for the attack, her escape, and the long trip to Middlebury, she probably never would've connected with Kyran, but she would rather it happened differently. Yet, she could never feel sorry for Kyran happening to her no matter what the circumstances. That one factor, and that one factor alone, made it all worthwhile: Kyran.

Kyran and their future together.

Memories swept past faster than the speed of light.

Adam. She remembered the decision she made, as well. At the precise moment when she discovered how much survival meant to her, she decided she'd leave Adam for good.

It saddened her. All that lost time. It shouldn't have ever happened, but there *were* some good times. Now it was too late to talk and explain, to make him understand. The notion stunned her into awareness.

The will to live extraordinarily seized her.

"No," she whispered, and screamed. Then, more urgently, "No!"

"I'm going to kill you, Bitch," Crater said. His voice was a low, guttural grumble. His lip curled. His ominous tone chilled her.

Victoria ran for him and lunged, but he was far too quick for her. He grabbed hold of her, and his rough hands fastened around her neck and squeezed. The was a sardonic gleam in his eyes. Her breathing stopped. She gagged and lashed at him repeatedly. Her eyes bulged in their sockets. She bucked and struggled to get away, emitting gurgling sounds. For a moment, Crater looked straight into her eyes and snickered.

***

Kyran heard Victoria scream and ran upstairs in the direction of the master bedroom. He found her in a struggle with a man, and he knew his only defense would be to react swiftly. He must think quickly, intelligently, and logically for he knew with the utmost certainty this man meant to destroy. His failure to control the situation not only jeopardized his life, but the life of the woman he loved, as well. Kyran grabbed the first thing he got his eyes on and rushed at him, brandishing the poker stick from the fireplace. He had no fear.

Victoria's attacker saw Kyran coming at him with the poker stick. He let go of Victoria and grabbed for his blade in his jacket pocket.

Kyran managed to raise the poker stick high above his head ready to bring it down hard. But it seemed this man had a sixth sense and knew what was happening even before it occurred. He was extremely quick and was on Kyran in an instant.

Brandishing his knife, the man backed Kyran into a corner, but Kyran didn't give up that easy.

The seriousness of the situation was increasing by the second. Reacting quickly was crucial to their survival.

Kyran summoned the animal hidden within himself. Regardless of how sane he was, he was ready and willing to release that animal in order to save them both. His adrenaline flowed. He was capable of anything right now. Although he never hurt any living thing in his entire life, if necessary, he would act as any animal would in self-defense. And this was without a doubt self-defense!

Before he could do anything else, the man lunged, but Kyran kicked up his leg, knocking the blade far out of reach on the hallway carpet. The intruder tackled Kyran down and whacked him. The struggle increased. Kyran's breath caught in his throat making him gag. Kyran was fast but not fast enough. The wild man was faster and better.

Time spun on maddeningly. Kyran fought with animal ferocity but couldn't score a single hit. He absolutely couldn't break the other's defenses to draw blood. He pushed himself up from the floor, only to be kicked in the face again, knocking him into the doorjamb in the process.

The intruder's lips were pulled back in a porthole-sized grin of rage. He threw a heavy statuette in Kyran's direction, missing and shattering the stained-glass window above his head. Kyran's heart thrummed with fright at the near miss.

* * *

Victoria screamed Kyran's name and rushed to pick up the blade from where it lay on the hallway carpet. Time was moving ever so swiftly, but she was moving fast, as well. She turned to see the man throw a might shove making Kyran fly backward, strike the wall, and tumble down the stairwell. He hit his head on the corner of the pointed banister, before rolling, then sliding to the bottom.

"No!" Victoria screamed. "You bastard!"

The man made it to his feet. Victoria quickly retrieved the knife and sprang forward. Pulling the blade from behind her back, using all the strength she could muster, Victoria plunged it into the man's chest as he lurched forward, swinging one muscular-built arm at her.

"Shit!" The tendons in his neck pulsated. "Iiiiii!" he shrieked, his expression of utter dumb surprise.

He fell headfirst down the stairwell, landing on top of Kyran. His right arm twisted oddly beneath him. He lay motionless.

Victoria ran over to where they both lay at the bottom of the stairs and pushed the heavy, boulder-like object that was the attacker off Kyran. She noticed Kyran struggle to open his eyes, but within seconds lose consciousness yet again.

She heard sirens in the distance, steadily drawing nearer. Concerned neighbors must have summoned the police after hearing Victoria's ear shattering screams, along with the cacophony of the breaking stained-glass window.

Victoria shuddered in revulsion at the sight of her attacker, and what she did to make him stop. She stood rooted to the spot on the hall carpet and couldn't move. Her legs were wobbly, but she was able to steady herself. Although she was dizzy, she didn't dare pass out. Kyran might be badly wounded or dead.

Dead. Somehow thinking the word made it reality. She was convinced it was truth.

She was suddenly overcome with remorse. Had she lost Kyran already after only just finding him? She was fortunate her obsession for him turned out so well. He could've turned out to be the opposite of what she imagined: lewd and stuck-up. Instead, in real-life, he was better than she ever dreamed up. Better in every respect. He was kind, loving and gentle. An intelligent man, and then some.

But now he was dead.

An unbearable sense of loss overwhelmed her. He was dead! The thought was devastating. Tears stung her eyes. She tried to smother her tears and anguish but could hold it in no longer. She rested her head on Kyran's chest.

"Kyran," she cried, "Why did you have to leave me?"

Victoria looked up and saw blood was splattered all over the front of Kyran's shirt. She immediately thought it was Kyran's. "Oh,

God!"

Did the attacker have another weapon and use it on Kyran? He must have.

She looked at the attacker's lifeless body and caught sight of blood still oozing from the open wound she herself inflicted on him. Somewhat relieved, she looked at Kyran's face. The blood had been smeared onto his shirt when the man fell on top of him.

He turned in the direction of her voice, and lifted his head, groaning in the progress, focusing his eyes on Victoria. She wept with relief.

"How could I have been so stupid?" he whispered; his voice raw with strain. A grimace of pain contorted his face. "You're hurt." Kyran noticed red bruises adorning the center of her neck.

Victoria nodded. She knew it would be sore and black and blue for a while, but eventually it would disappear, leaving behind no scars and nothing to show it ever even happened. The emotional scars would eventually heal, but for now, she needed to fend with a throat that burned as if she'd gargled with Drano.

"W-Who was he?" Kyran asked.

"The man responsible for putting me in the hospital. I remember him now. I remember it all now." Her voice was tight, choked.

Kyran tried to speak again, but Victoria hushed him. She wiped the top of his eyebrow with the bottom of her sweatshirt. The bleeding stopped, but there was a wide-open gash approximately six inches long marking the top of his forehead above his left eye where he hit his head. He would most certainly retain a scar. "I'm not the one we have to worry about," she said.

Screaming sirens, closer now, were followed by screeching tires.

Victoria proceeded to get up. "Rest, Darling. I'll be right back," she said.

***

Newspaper reporters and cameramen were all over, swarming around the policemen at work. Behind the yellow police line, a local television network's crew was preparing to tape a story to be aired on the late-night news program. Some of the curious bystanders stood pointing. Others took cell phone videos of their own, hoping to sell it to the first high offer. The entire entourage of people could be seen and heard talking and laughing considering the circumstances of their coming together. Others walked up to join in on the joke. As time went by, eventually the disappointed crowd, failing to find out any of the morbid details, would begin to disperse, but for now the scene had their full attention.

It was raining again, something which Kyran and Victoria became quite accustomed to, but it didn't seem to displease or affect the onlookers who gathered to gape at the scene. Everyone and their brother fought to get their face on camera. The scene was a haze of words and dialogue.

Uniformed officers attempted to control the gathered crowd Victoria overheard her neighbor loudly expressing her opinion, "I'm Gladys Stagman. I live right next door. They always seemed like such a nice couple."

Victoria snickered and thought, *little does anyone know she's a drunk with a husband who beats her.*

The ambulance attendants opened the rear doors and carefully loaded Kyran in the back. Victoria slid in beside him.

As the ambulance drove off, sirens blaring into the night, headed in the direction of St. Anthony's Hospital in Warwick, New York, Victoria crouched next to the stretcher where Kyran rested. She was in a daze, her eyes distant, unblinking and tired.

"I love you, you know," she whispered.

She rested her hand along his cheek and base of his chin and placed a soft kiss on his lips. He slowly opened his eyes and gazed up at her. She smiled a little, tears still glistening in the corner of her eyes.

Chapter 9

"If thou must love me, let it be for naught

except for love's sake only."

--Elizabeth Barett Browning

The weather changed dramatically. For the first day in weeks, the sun peeked through the clouds, valiantly announcing its presence, and decided to stay, as if to say, "The worst is over. Now onto brighter days."

Kyran honked the horn and watched as Victoria strode down the walkway headed in his direction, carrying what looked to be a book and a small, wrapped package. She waved a delicate hand, which was long and thin with square-shaped fingernails, probably filed that way to perfection. She was wearing a sweater of bright fuchsia and black stonewashed jeans. Her skin shined a healthy pink glow. Her way of walking was stylish, but natural, brisk and slightly springy. She seemed to be quickly gliding in a step of dance. Her small head with its dirty-blonde hair flying freely bristled with life. When she finally slipped into the passenger side of the car with as much grace as she did when walking, Kyran noticed the smile of her vulnerable hazel eyes.

He basked in the wonder of her and considered himself extremely fortunate to have found her. Considering the previous week's events, he came close to losing her altogether, and it scared him half to death. It was sad how they got together. Because of Adam's death, they were now together permanently.

The police told them the dead man, the attacker, was Emilio Rodriguez, a guy with a record a mile long. They were trying to track him down for years to no avail. Although they were able to connect him to numerous crimes, they'd always been unable to apprehend him. After Victoria was finally able to explain what happened during her abduction, the police were able to connect him to a string of other recent murders, which took place along the same route he traveled. Careful investigation revealed he was responsible for them all.

"You look beautiful enough to eat," he said kiddingly, affectionately.

Blushing, she responded, "And this is just leftovers."

"What's the book for?" he asked.

"I wanted to show you the journal I'm writing," she answered. "I've written down absolutely everything I can remember from when I was little on up. I want to make sure if it ever happens again that I forget, I can read the journal to help me remember. I don't ever want to go through what I did again."

He smiled and patted her hand.

"Believe me. I'll make sure you don't forget," he said. Their lives were drastically altered, but infinitely entwined. Having found each other, they also found the will to go on.

Victoria turned and touched the beginning of the scar developing above Kyran's left eyebrow. When the doctor sewed up the stitches, he discussed plastic surgery with Kyran so no scar would remain, but Kyran decided against it. Although it was a sad reminder of the incident, it was a beautiful reminder of the union between the two of them. She joked about how it looked rugged and distinguished, offering yet another persona for his profession.

She smiled her amazingly beautiful smile.

"Ready?" he asked. She nodded in affirmation.

They didn't speak as Kyran drove, and within moments, he was parked in front of the same memorial park, Woodbourne Park, where not too long ago, they went to discuss their future—one they were sure was nonexistent then. After surviving one of the most profound experiences, they were returning to the same place to discuss a future they were certain of now. They got out of the car and walked over to the water fountain. Their arms were around each other's waists as they watched the water flowing in ringlets.

Victoria pulled the tiny wrapped package from her pants pocket. Kyran almost forgot he saw her carrying it to the car.

"What is it?" he asked.

"Open it," she responded.

It was haphazardly wrapped, as if she'd done it in a hurry. He carefully opened it, relishing every moment, and found a single gold band. Kyran looked over at her, confused.

"It's my wedding band," she informed him. "I thought this would be the perfect place to put the past to rest. All I'll ever need to know I can find in my journal. I need to make new memories. Better ones."

"Are you sure?" he asked.

She nodded.

"Good idea."

Victoria watched as Kyran tossed the gold band into the water. One single *kurplop,* and it floated gently to the bottom.

ABOUT THE AUTHOR

Eleanor Wagner is married with two children currently residing in the beautiful countryside of Wantage, New Jersey in Sussex County. Born and raised in Throggs Neck in the Bronx, she attended St. Frances de Chantal and moved onto Cardinal Spellman High School, graduating with the well-known class of 1983.

She graduated from Grace Institute in Manhattan and spent her earlier years working as an Administrative Assistant in the Downtown area of New York while continuously writing in her spare time.

While putting her career aside to raise her small children, she became a children's party clown, Pennywhistle, so she could safely release her *inner child* by providing a musical, interactive program for children, utilizing her love of music and singing.

She studied at the Institute of Children's Literature where she learned how to write for children and teenagers, earning her diploma in 1993.

It was in and around this time she decided to take on the task of putting a book idea down in manuscript form. *Dream a Little Dream* is the fruit of her efforts and is her first published novel.

Made in the USA
Middletown, DE
17 June 2025

77001996R00103